I0654284

Doubting

Thomas

Nurse Hal Among The Amish Series

Book 7

Fay Risner

ISBN 13 9780982459577
ISBN 10 0982459572

Booksbyfay Publisher
fayrisner@netins.net
Publisher, author and Editor Fay Risner

Eye has not seen, ear has not heard, nor has it dawned on man what God has prepared for those who love him.
1 Corinthians 2:9

Reviews
The Courting Buggy

I have read the whole series of Nurse Hal. If you like Amish fiction I highly recommend you get the whole series, I just finished "The Courting Buggy" and it is Great. It is a story of a English woman who married a Amish man that has children. This book has everything. Humor, romance, death and birth. I cannot tell you how great this is but encourage you to read the series. You will not be sorry. Fay Risner is a excellent writer of Amish books. I am waiting for more of Nurse Hal.

Christmas Traditions - An Amish Love Story

This book is an informative, intelligent piece from a human interest point of view. Your writing is atmospheric and your narrative comes across as natural, believable and very vivid. Margaret is already so likeable but I'm not so sure of Levi. I think any story which helps its characters to emerge out of their self indulgent ways to great understanding and a fuller compassionate existence is worth the read.

Promise Is A Promise - Book One

You have done it again! This is a well written, intricate and richly detailed tapestry of Amish life. Maybe it's just my personal preference but I do love stories like this about a way of life based on faith, convictions and honesty. It's a beautiful story that had my rapt attention all the way through. A compelling read that I found hard to put down once started.

Charlie Courtland host of http://www.bitsybling.wordpress.com Growing up in the Mid West I loved the style and tone of the story and scenery. No purple prose or overly nostalgic descriptions but rather a simple and honest portrayal of daily life. Each character is original and thoughtfully developed. I whole heartedly enjoyed this Amish tale and believed the contrast between the Plain and English, but also how it is possible to live together with understanding, honesty and acceptance. The story is not overtly religious but rather focuses on the complexities of relationships and because of this drew me into the Lapp family. Bitsy's Rating" 4 stars

If you would like to leave a review about any of my books go to one of the places they are sold. I always appreciate reviews from my readers.

Fay Risner's books are sold by her at her home, on Amazon, B&N, Smashwords, Kindle and Nook. Email her at fayrisner@netins.net to purchase a signed book.

Nurse Hal Among The Amish Series

A Promise Is A Promise   Doubting Thomas
The Rainbow's End
Hal's Worldly Temptations
As Her Name Is So Is Redbird
Emma's Gossamer Dreams
The Courting Buggy

Amazing Gracie Historical Mystery Series

Neighbor Watchers   Poor Defenseless Addie
Specious Nephew
The Country Seat Killer
The Chance Of A Sparrow
Moser Mansion Ghosts
Locked Rock, Iowa Hatchet Murders

Westerns

Stringbean Hooper Westerns   Tread Lightly Sibby
The Dark Wind Howls Over Mary   Ella Mayfields' Pawpaw Miltia
Small Feet's Many Moon Journey

Christmas books

Christmas Traditions - An Amish Love Story
Leona's Christmas Bucket List
Christmas With Hover Hill

Romance

Sunset to Sunrise On Buttercup Lane by Connie Risner

Children Books

My Children Are More Precious Than Gold
Mr. Quacker The Odd Duck   Spooks In Claiborne Mansion

Nonfiction about Alzheimer's disease

Open A Window - Caregiver Handbook
Hello Alzheimer's Goodbye Dad-author's true story

Cookbook

Midwest Favorite Lamb Recipes

Military

Redcatcher MP (Vietnam War) by Mickey Bright

Then Jesus said to Thomas, "Put your finger here. See my hands. Reach out your hand and put it into my side. Stop doubting and believe.

Thomas said to him, "My Lord and my God."

Then Jesus told him, "Because you have seen me you have believed; blessed are those that have not seen and yet have believed.

John 20: 27-29

Chapter 1

That Sunday morning's worship service was at Elmo Zook's house. Bishop Elton Bontrager read resolution seven of The Dordrecht Confession of Faith to Emma Lapp and twelve others joining the church. "Concerning holy baptism, we confess that penitent believers, who, through faith, regeneration, and the renewing of the Holy Ghost, are made one with God, and are written in heaven, must, upon such Scriptural confession of faith, and renewing of life, be baptized with water. In the most worthy name of the Father, and of the Son, and of the Holy Ghost, according to the command of Christ, and the teaching, example, and practice of the apostles, to the burying of their sins. Thus be incorporated into the communion of the saints; henceforth to learn to observe all things which the Son of God has taught, left, and commanded His disciples."

Emma sighed, thinking about how happy she felt now. She'd finally committed herself to be a member of the Amish faith for the rest of her life. This June day was a momentous one for her. She'd made it through her conversion ceremony. Now another big life changing moment was coming, her wedding. Adam Keim and she could make plans now that she was truly Amish forever.

The day's heated breeze hadn't cooled off much after dark.

1

Emma leaned against the buggy seat and pushed a few sweaty, light brown curls back under her prayer cap. Before her glowed the buggy headlights, Behind her, red lights reflected on the road from the tail lights. She fanned her face with her hand as she tried to relax. Sophie's soft hoof beats and the crunch of rock under the wheels filled the moonlit silence.

She was dying to discuss their wedding with Adam, but she hadn't worked up the nerve yet. This change in her life would be as serious as joining the church. She'd move from her family home with a familiar routine. Until she got used to her new life living with Adam was the unknown. She'd dreamed of making a home with this man for several years, but now that the time was closing in on her, she was uneasy.

Her gray-green eyes warmed as she studied her husband-to-be. He was only an inch or two taller than her, strong as an ox, with a round, pleasant face, a stocky body and work worn hands. An industrious man, Adam had his own carpentry business complete with a shop. He made a good enough income to support a family.

She considered it a blessing that her father, John Lapp, and Adam were very much alike. Nothing ruffled either man for long since they were filled with a God given calmness she'd never have.

Emma admired Adam's steely resolve when he quietly took what life threw at him and found his way through the problems. Perhaps, that purpose filled demeanor came from the fact he was born with what was considered a big set back for most people. Adam couldn't talk.

Emma hadn't seen his speechlessness as a problem between them while she was growing up around him. He communicated volumes with a look or hand gesture. If that didn't work, he always had a writing pad and pen in his shirt pocket.

She smiled and put her hand on Adam's arm. "Did you hear how off key Freda Manwiller was tonight at the singing?"

Emma was glad for the full moon. The glow helped her see Adam's responses. He shook his head no.

Emma giggled. "Take it from me. Freda could not carry a

tune in an empty milk pail. Gute thing the rest of us sang loud enough to cover her voice."

Adam focused on her with narrowed eyes.

Emma sobered up quickly. "What is it?" They had been together so long she usually read what was on his mind. "Ach, you are thinking I am making fun of Freda."

Adam gave a slight nod.

Emma turned serious. "I am sorry. I did not mean to be hurtful. If you do not want me to, I will not bring Freda's singing up again."

Adam's brown eyes held a flicker of amusement before he nodded yes.

Emma took a deep breath and folded her hands together. She might as well take the plunge. No better time than this while they were alone to get the subject she really needed to discuss out in the open. "Gute! We do have more important things to discuss than the singing. Since I am a member of the church now, we can plan our wedding if you are ready."

Adam gave her a loving glance and an emphatic yes shake of his head.

What a relief this was. Adam made talking about the wedding easier for Emma. She laughed as she slapped him playfully on the shoulder. "Gute! I am glad I finally picked a conversation you liked."

Adam pulled back on the lines to slow Sophie and turned off on Bender Creek Road. He stopped around the bend in the dirt road and flipped off the headlights. With his attention on Emma, he waited.

"Well, I have given this much thought already. The first thing is tell our families we are ready to marry. My parents need to be told so they can start planning the wedding for September."

Adam stared straight ahead, bunching and unbunching the lines in his hands.

"Why are you suddenly so nervous already? Will that be too soon to marry? It is only a little over three months away. Is setting the wedding in September too soon for you?"

This time Adam didn't look at her when he nodded no.

"All recht. Is it that you are scared of the details that have to be worked out?"

Adam smiled at her weakly as he held out his hand with an exaggerated tremor.

"And do you think I am *not* nervous? This is a big step we are taking, but we have been ready for a long time. Talking to our families will be easy. They are eager for us to announce our marriage," Emma said.

Adam nodded in agreement.

"Gute! We can talk to my parents tonight when we get to my house," Emma suggested.

Adam's face scrunched up like a dried prune.

"There you go again, looking like you are in pain. Relax. This will be the easiest part of the next few months," Emma warned.

Adam wavered his hand as a question.

"You know it will be."

Adam pulled the pad and pen out of his shirt pocket. He held them close to him so he could see in the dark as he wrote, "We do not have to say anything tonight. I will get Deacon Yutzy to be my Schteckliman. He can go talk to your parents."

"Nah, alls you are doing is getting out of facing my daed and Hallie. We are not a shy young couple. You do not need a go-between for this like most couples use.

Maybe we could marry on September fifteenth. That is my twentieth birthday. Hallie and I should have the details done by then. But we should wait until you and I talk to Daed and Hallie. If that date does not work for them, any day close to it will be all recht. Ain't so?"

Adam nodded, giving her a wide smile.

Emma scooted close and wrapped her arm around his. "I know. The sooner the better as long as you do not have to do the planning. That way you might just barely manage to make it through the next few months and through the wedding ceremony."

He nodded emphatically, hugged Emma and turned on the

buggy lights. Emma laid her head on his shoulder. Sophie poked along the back road beside Bender Creek to the intersection with the main road.

As Adam turned Sophie into the Lapp driveway, Emma teased, "Gute thing you decided the sooner we get the talk to my parents over with the better for our nerves. We will be standing before my parents in two minutes."

Adam's shoulders sagged as he turned a dispirited, puppy face on Emma. After he climbed out of the buggy, he stared toward the house and gave a deep, silent sigh. Giggling as nervously as a school girl, Emma grabbed Adam's hand and pulled him toward the house. "You will live through this moment. I promise."

The Lapp farm was dark and sleepy. Milk cows were silhouetted mounds bedded down in the pen by the milk room. The horses, black blobs, slept on their feet. The only bright spot was the living room window's warm, welcoming glow.

Emma opened the screen door, stepped in and glanced around the quiet room. Daed sat in his rocker, reading his bible. It occurred to Emma that her father's dark hair had a few streaks of gray in it these days. Hallie's head was bent over her sewing. Her red hair showed through the black prayer cap she wore, making for a bright combination. Hallie was putting a patch on a trouser knee for sixteen years old Daniel. That was a never ending job. No sight of her brothers, but they couldn't be too far behind. Her little sisters, Redbird and Beth, must be in bed. This was a good time to talk to her parents while they were by themselves.

"You're back already. My, the night has passed fast. Where are Noah and Daniel?" Hal laid the trousers in the wicker basket on top the other clothes to be mended.

"Close behind us, ain't so?" Emma glanced over her shoulder at Adam.

He nodded an agreement.

"You have a gute evening?" Hal stuck her needle in the black thread spool and nestled the spool beside the scissors in the basket.

5

"We did," Emma said, clasping her hands in front of her.

Hal patted the couch beside her. "For goodness sakes, don't just stand there. Come over here and sit by me. I want to hear how the singing went tonight. Many kids there?"

They sat down, but Emma didn't answer. She was too busy biting her lower lip as she looked at Adam.

Hal leaned forward and smiled at Adam. He gave her a trembling, return smile. Something definitely was amiss. Hal could sense it. She studied Emma's usually tan face. Her complexion paled enough that the freckles popped out around her nose. Adam held his midsection tightly like he had a queasy stomach.

Hal gave John a concerned look. He frowned as he nodded in agreement. He felt it, too. Hal twisted toward the quiet couple. "You are worrying me. Something must be wrong. Was ist letz?"

Emma licked her lips and turned to Adam for support. "Nothing is wrong. We had a talk on the way home, Adam and me."

Adam put his finger to her lips to stop her. He took the notepad and pen out of his pocket. They waited while he wrote on it. Adam turned the pad to Emma and raised an eyebrow for approval. Then he pointed at John. Emma smiled sheepishly as she nodded agreement.

Adam got up from the couch, tore off the paper and handed it to John. After reading the note, John gave Adam a wide grin. "Jah, Adam."

Now that the moment was over, a huge weight lifted off his sagging shoulders. Adam stood taller and straighter.

"Will someone please tell me what's going on?" Hal barked, looking from the men to Emma and back.

"Daed, read Hallie Adam's note," Emma instructed.

"John Lapp, I, Adam Keim, want to ask you for permission to marry your daughter, Emma Lapp." He smiled at Emma. "You have Hal and my permission to marry. We very much want this man as our son-in-law." John held out his hand to shake hands with Adam.

Hal brought her hands up to the sides of her face. "Oh my! Emma, it seemed to me this day was slow in coming. And again, I figured it would be soon after you joined the church. Not the very day though. That I didn't see coming." Hal laughed as she hugged Emma. She went to Adam and give him a sturdy hug. When she stepped back, she looked at him earnestly. "You're like a member of this family already. It will be great to finally make you officially part of the Lapp family, sealed with a wedding."

Adam gave a silent laugh and wrote, "You do understand I am not becoming a Lapp. Emma is becoming a Keim."

Hal laughed as she read the note to John. With a teasing warning in her voice, she said, "Silly, I know that, but you once said we hadn't adopted you. Seems to me, marrying into this family is just as gute. Take my word for it, we will have plans for you, Adam Keim."

Adam gave Emma a nonplussed glance.

"Ach, Adam, Hallie is teasing, ain't so, Hallie?" Emma asked tentatively.

Hal clasped her hands together and winked at Adam. "Well, maybe to start with. Adam is safe for now, because we'll be busy with far too many plans for this wedding. Have you picked a date yet?"

Emma said, "September fifteenth is my twentieth birthday. I wondered if we could get married on that day, but if that is not possible, we can pick another date that works for you."

"John, what do you think?" Hal asked.

"What Emma and Adam wants is all recht with me," John said agreeably.

"Gute, then the date is agreed on if it works for the bishop. You should talk to him soon so another couple doesn't get that date." Hal went silent and stared off into space.

Emma imagined wheels turning in her stepmother's mind, like those in the alarm clock. "Hallie, what are you thinking?"

"I'm counting up the days in my head. This is the first of June. Lots of details to work out by mid September. Oh dear, I hope I'm up to this task."

"I will help you, Hallie. We will do this together," Emma encouraged.

"We need to make a list so we can mark the details off as we finish them," Hal said, starting for the kitchen. "I'll get a pad and pen."

Emma grabbed her arm. "We will do that but not until tomorrow. It is too late tonight to think about wedding details. We need to be rested so we have clear heads."

Hal's parents, Jim and Nora Lindstrom, received a letter a few days later about Emma and Adam's fall wedding. They were eager to drive from Titonka to the Lapp farm as soon as possible.

Nora asked her sister, Tootie, if she wanted to go with them again. Tootie hesitated while she gave traveling south into Amish country some thought. She had sad memories from the last time she visited the Lapps.

For some reason, these days she didn't always have a lot of energy. She knew the stay at the Lapp farm would be a long one. All summer from the sounds of things, and that would be tiring. Then again, she liked Emma and Adam an awful lot. She felt as if she should be at their wedding, and she'd like to be there. So in the end, Tootie talked herself into going with Jim and Nora.

As soon as they finished packing, Jim headed Nora and Tootie to the car, and they were on the road. They stopped for lunch at a roadside diner. Jim stopped twice to gas the car at Casey Stores where they could use the restroom and get a bottle of pop. By late afternoon, they were near Wickenburg.

"Tootie, you've been quiet for miles. Are you asleep back there?" Nora Lindstrom twisted in the seat to look over her shoulder at her sister.

Tootie's curly, short hair had less gray in it than her straight, feathered cut. Nora suspected Tootie colored her hair, but Tootie wouldn't tell. Most people commented they looked a lot alike, but Nora couldn't see it. Tootie was shorter than her by a head.

8

"I'm not asleep. Just don't have a reason to talk. Haven't seen anything interesting out my window to mention that I didn't see when we made the trip the last time," groused Tootie. "How much longer until we get to the Lapp Farm?"

"Maybe an hour," Jim Lindstrom said, pressing his aching, broad shoulders against the seat and massaging the back of his neck just below his white hair with his left hand.

"Tootie, you better relax while you can. Hallie's letter says she's going to need a lot of help, preparing for Emma's wedding. She intends to put us to work as soon as we get there," Nora forewarned.

"You said you'd read her letter to me. You never did," Tootie said in a pouting tone.

"Sorry, I forgot. I brought the letter with me." Nora rifled through her purse. "Ah, here it is." She unfolded the letter and underscored each line with a fingertip as she read out loud.

Dear Mom and Dad,
Greeting to you on this lovely summer day.
We want to share our wonderful news from the Lapp farm. Emma and Adam are getting married. You know how delighted we are. Finally, this young man is going to be part of our family. Of course, he has seemed like family for a long time already. That's the good news.

Not so good news is, Emma and I have so much to do to prepare for the wedding we don't know where to start. I can't remember when I've been so nervous about the success of any one event. I'm afraid we're going to need lots of help if you two are willing to come lend a hand. We will be expecting two hundred plus guests.

If the wedding preparations weren't enough to keep me busy, taking care of Redbird and Beth is a challenge. They're quite a pair of mischievous, energetic three year olds but better than when they were in their terrible twos.

What a difference six months makes. One afternoon, Emma set the egg basket too close to the edge of the table and went back outside to water the chickens. She was gone longer than she meant to be. She had to break up a squabble between Tom Turkey and the dog. They were both after the same cold biscuit.

While we weren't looking, the girls pulled the basket off the table onto the floor. What eggs didn't break, I'm sure the girls helped crack by playing ball with them.

It took Emma and me both to clean up the mess and the girls. By the time I bathed the girls, Emma had the kitchen floor spotless again. You know how particular Emma is about her clean floors. It took her a little while to get her sense of humor back about the mess and the loss of all those good eggs. We're very glad to see Redbird and Beth are passed that stage.

John plans to butcher the fattened hog just before the wedding day. Pulled pork sandwiches are on the menu for the wedding lunch. That's a big project and mean hours of cooking pork. Emma will pick women in the community to help cook the other food, including fried chicken. I understand that's the way it works. We will be glad for all their help.

Now that I've shared our news, I must get busy. We want you to be here for the wedding and please pass our invitation on to Aunt Tootie. We want her to share this special day with us, the Lord willing and if she is up to it.

Keep Emma and me in your prayers that all goes well as we plan this wonderful event. Emma and I agree there isn't a need for us or you to worry about praying for John and Adam. As with most men, Emma says the men are mistakenly going on the premise what will be will be. That means they assume Emma and I will handle everything important so that lets them off the hook. Ha!

With All Our Love and Christ's Blessing On Both Of You,

Hallie and the Lapp family

Nora grinned at Jim. "Isn't that a funny story about Redbird and Beth getting into the eggs?"

Jim chuckled. "Sounds like the little girls are starting out just

10

like Hallie did at that age. Remember what a handful she was?"

"Indeed I do, and I'll remind her when I get a chance. Help me think of some of the mischievous things she did. I'm sure I won't remember them all," Nora said.

Tootie huffed. "Are we going to hear a bunch more of these cute baby stories while we're at the farm?"

"Ah, Tootie! Don't you like cute baby stories?" Nora asked.

"Well, maybe one now and then is okay, but too many of them aren't cute anymore. After awhile, they're just plain tiresome," Tootie complained.

"You shouldn't be that way. Those girls are your great nieces," scolded Nora.

"All I'm saying is cute baby stories should be short and told very infrequently as far as I'm concerned," Tootie declared.

"Don't worry about it. Hal will be too busy to tell many stories. She's going to be planning the wedding," Jim said.

"That's very true. That's why I want to get to the farm as quickly as we can so we can help," Nora said.

"If John figures on butchering a hog for the meal, he and the boys will need help. I haven't helped butcher since I was a young man. I sure want to get in on that," Jim said eagerly.

Chapter 2

Paper rustling noises came from the back seat. Nora scolded, "Tootie, are you eating another candy bar? We'll be eating supper with Hallie and her family soon. You know how much food Hallie and Emma feed us. Can't you wait?"

"I'm not eating. I'm reading, and I don't like what I just read. If we weren't so far from home, I'd make Jim turn around and take me back. You didn't tell me before we started I'd have to work on this trip. Come to think of it, I didn't know I'd have to work the last time either. Look how that turned out." Tootie made protesting, tisking noises. "I'd say this visit is going to be worse."

"What on earth are you talking about?" Nora asked.

Tootie droned, "Many hands are needed to prepare mountains of food for a wedding. A woman, especially adept to baking, was asked to make four hundred doughnuts. Aunts on the bride's mother's side make most of the cookies and wedding nothings also known as Knee Patches. Those are thin, sweet fried pastries sprinkled with confectioner's sugar.

The bride's mother is responsible for orchestrating the work before the wedding, but she appoints an organizer, usually a close relative to be in charge on the wedding day." The elderly woman stopped to take a breath before she said, "Close relatives to Emma are you and me, Nora. Let me tell you, I don't know nothing about making Wedding Nothings. You're on your own when they ask for fried pastries."

"How do you know this stuff?"

"I'm reading it."

"You didn't bring that old Amish book with you?" Nora snapped.

"Not the one you mean. I bought a book on Amish weddings so I'd know what happens. It's called *The Amish Wedding and other special occasions of the Old Order Communities*. It's a good thing I did. Now I know what we're in for since we're the bride's Aunt and Grandma."

"For goodness sakes! A little work won't hurt you. Don't you know doing nothing will wear you out faster than keeping busy?"

"Says you, Sister. Anyhow, I see nothing wrong with being informed about the Amish customs. After all, we'll be rubbing elbows with a bunch of Amish at the wedding," Tootie defended.

Nora huffed in annoyance.

Jim said, "Now, Nora, I don't see what bringing that book with her will hurt."

Tootie perked up. "Thank you, Jim."

Nora threw Tootie's words back at her. "All right, I'm outnumbered. Let me tell you this. If you get that book out in front of Hallie's family, it should only be for a short time and very infrequently."

For the rest of the trip, Tootie stayed quiet in the back seat. Nora peeked over her shoulder several times to see if her sister was awake. Tootie chose to keep quiet and occupy herself by staring out the window.

Jim turned off the pavement onto a gravel road south of Wickenburg. He drove past picturesque farms, rolling pastures and forests now familiar to them. As he drove by the turn off to Bender Creek road, Jim announced, "Passing Lover's Lane. We'll be at the Lapp farm shortly, ladies." He glanced at his wrist watch. "Four o'clock. Just in time for me to help with milking."

When at last they reached Hallie Lapp's home, Jim pulled

into the driveway and parked. The family's cream colored dog crawled out from under the enclosed buggy in the lean-to and raced to meet the car. He stopped at the edge of the lawn and turned toward the house. His head lifted high, he howled one of his finest baying alerts to the Lapp family to tell them company had arrived.

The dog wanted to do some greeting of his own. He ran to the car, jumped up and peered in the back window at Tootie. She gasped when his head came so close even though glass was between them. The dog gave her a toothy grin and smeared the window with his wet nose, trying to get at her.

"Look how big that dog has gotten. He sure has grown since the last time we saw him," Jim declared.

"I hope the boys get out here soon and hold onto him. If he's loose, I'm not getting out of the car. He might knock us down," Tootie grumbled.

"Now, Tootie, don't complain about that dog. Hallie's family likes him, but I must admit Jim the dog is too big to let jump on us," Nora admonished.

Tootie gave the dog her meanest glare as she slapped the window, trying to scare him into getting down. "Jim, when he was a puppy, I liked him, too. Now not so much."

"I'll ask the boys to keep the dog away from the car so you two can get out," Jim growled. As the Lapp family gathered at the edge of the driveway, he climbed out and greeted them. "Hi, folks." The dog brushed against his leg. Jim bent and patted his head. Satisfied he'd had his share of attention, the dog trotted over to stand by Noah and Daniel.

"We're so glad you made it safely," Hal cried, giving him a big hug, which included hugging blonde haired Beth in her arms.

John shook hands with Jim while Redbird wiggled in his arms, trying to get down. Jim patted Redbird on her red head. "Hello, sweet thing."

Hal motioned toward the car for Nora and Tootie to join them. They shook their heads no. "Why aren't Mom and Aunt Tootie getting out?"

Jim snickered. "They're afraid of the dog. He took a liking to Tootie already. Tried to kiss her through the window. Boys, do you still call your dog Biscuit or have you given him another name?"

Noah ducked his head sheepishly." Nah, he is still Biscuit."

"Good enough. Could you distract Biscuit until we get those two old ladies in the house?"

"Sure, Dawdi," Daniel said, grinning. He walked into the driveway, called and patted his leg. "Here, Biscuit. Come." The dog loped toward him. Daniel grabbed him around the neck. "Now what do I do with him?"

"Shut him in the barn for awhile," John suggested.

Noah followed Daniel so he could open the barn door. He whispered, "Aendi Tootie should not complain about our dog. Her kisses are just as wet as Biscuit's."

As soon as Daniel shut the barn door on the dog, Biscuit howled in protest. The boys walked back to stand with the others, and Hal beckoned the women in the car with her hand. Nora and Tootie rushed from the car and hugged Hal and John. Nora gave Redbird and Beth a kiss on their out turned cheeks.

Tootie did likewise. Redbird giggled. Beth frowned slightly. Both girls instantly wiped their cheeks with their chubby hands.

"Give me a hug, bride-to-be," Nora said, throwing her arms around Emma.

"Me next," said Tootie, standing right behind Nora for her turn.

"My word," Nora said, inspecting Noah and Daniel. "I can't get over how much you boys have grown since the last time we were here. Noah, you are so tall. Are you eighteen yet?"

"Jah, Mammi," Noah said, giving her a bashful smile.

Jim patted Noah's shoulder. "Say, how is the courting buggy holding up? I figure you might be giving it a good workout by now."

Noah blushed. "Ach, nah, I share with Daniel. For the singings, we go together and take turns driving. The courting buggy is fine."

"Depends if Noah has a date or not, whether we go together," Daniel added unenthusiastically.

Jim put his arm around Daniel's shoulders. "Ah, ha. Well, by the next time we visit, I predict you'll be using the buggy for dates, too. How's my horse?"

"Mike is gute, Dawdi."

"Jah, we use him all the time. Mike pulls all recht now," Noah added, referring to the horse's traffic fright when Jim first bought him.

"You boys suppose I could put in my bid to take the buggy out now and then while I'm here?"

"Sure, any time you want," Noah said.

"Use it as much as you want, Dawdi," Daniel added. "Just say the word, and we will hitch it up to Mike for you."

Jim winked at them. "Good deal. I figured I'd take you grandma for a ride in it one of these days."

Tootie frowned at the barking noises coming from the barn. "Thank you, boys, for shutting up your dog. I just didn't want him to bounce on Nora and me. He might knock us down." She searched the area around them. "Where is that overly friendly turkey right now?"

Hal laughed. "No way to tell. He shows up when we least expect it."

"That's what I'm afraid might happen," Tootie said, causing them to laugh. "We better get inside before Tom appears unless you boys want to shut him up, too."

Company meant fixing extra food for meals. While the women worked in the kitchen, most of the talk was about the coming wedding. That evening, Tootie washed the dishes, and Emma dried. Hal put away the leftovers, and Nora washed off the counters and tables. It was as though Nora and Tootie had never left. They settled so easily into their old routine.

"Are you giving up teaching school now that you're getting married?" Tootie asked as she rubbed a plate with the dish cloth.

"Nah, I will teach, but I need the month of September off for the wedding and about two weeks of visiting which is our way.

16

I hope Ellen Miller will substitute teach for me. She was the teacher before me so she is not a stranger to the job."

Tootie asked, "Emma, have you picked your bridesmaids yet?"

"Jah, if you mean my newehockers?"

"I don't know. Do I?" Tootie asked, looking at Hal for help.

"They aren't called bridesmaids. The two couples in the wedding party are called attendants in English," Hal explained.

"One of my attendants is Katie Yost and the other one is Jenny Yoder. Do either of you remember my friends?" Emma asked.

Nora said, "Yes, I do but I'm sure they've grown up just like you and the boys. I probably wouldn't recognize them now."

"Jah, they have grown up. Sunday is the next worship service. I will introduce Aendi Tootie and you to them after I ask them to be my attendants," Emma said.

Tootie stopped washing a pot to stare at Emma. "You mean they don't know yet?"

"Not yet. Hallie and I just finished making a list of wedding plans. Telling my attendants is next on the list. They will need time to make their dresses as soon as I buy the material. We do not discuss the wedding with anyone else for a couple of months yet," Emma warned.

"Why not, dear?" Nora asked.

"It is our way. The bishop will not let the deacon publish the wedding announcement until the Sunday worship service in September two weeks before our wedding date. My father will invite everyone at that service. Once that is done, we can talk about the wedding and ask people to help us," Emma said. "Until then we will be spending the time getting ready for the wedding by ourselves."

"Oh, dear me. I need to get my Amish book on special occasions out and start reading again," Tootie exclaimed. "There's so much about how an Amish wedding works I don't understand yet. Nora, you better read the book, too."

Nora hung her dishcloth over the line behind the stove to dry. "No thanks. I think I'd rather ask questions. I'm finding out enough that way to suit me."

Tootie made a huffing sound.

Emma felt sorry for her. Mammi picked on her sister too much, and Tootie just wanted to help. "Maybe I should read your book, Aendi. I hate to think there is something I missed while we are planning this wedding. I want everything to be just recht."

Tootie was all smiles at that suggestion.

Nora slipped close to Emma and hissed, "You shouldn't encourage her. You will be sorry."

"Where will you live?" Tootie asked.

"Adam plans to remodel the open area above his shop into an apartment. That is only three miles from here so we will always be close by."

"Sounds handy, Adam that close to work, and you near your family," Nora said.

"Sure," Emma said.

She'd been busy working on wedding plans with Hallie, and today, she'd enjoyed visiting with her grandparents and aunt. All of a sudden at the mention of Adam, Emma wondered why she hadn't seen him since the last worship service over a week ago. She was surprised Adam didn't come for supper tonight to visit her company.

The rest of the week passed without seeing Adam. Emma was anxious for the next worship service so she could spend the afternoon with him. She hoped he hadn't become ill from so much work and not enough sleep.

The service was at Moses and Stella Strutt's farm. While the young women were waiting their turn to go inside, Emma told Katie and Jennie she wanted to talk to them. She led the way to a quiet spot in the yard, well aware the other young women watched them leave. They would be very curious now and trying to guess among themselves what was going on.

"Was ist letz?" The tall, willowy built girl's blue eyes seemed troubled as she looked down at Emma.

Emma giggled. Her tan face reddened, making her freckles darken. "Jenny Yoder, nothing is the matter. I have some gute news for both of you, and something I want to ask you where none of the others can hear me."

That made Katie Yost big blue eyes twinkle "What?"

"Adam and I are getting married in September on my birthday," Emma said softly.

The excited girls did a three way hug.

"We are so happy for you." Katie's pale cheeks flushed at the news as she added, "And I am a bit jealous."

"Why should you be? Levi Yoder is a great man," Emma said.

Jenny added, "I will agree with that since he is my brother."

"Jah, but sometimes, I worry I will end up a maidel before Levi decides to propose," Katie said.

"At least you have a sweetheart. I have yet to find me one," Jenny quipped.

Emma looked toward the house. The men had started to walk inside, and Adam was among them. "We have to go in soon. Before we do, I want to ask both of you if you will be my attendants."

Katie clapped her hands. "Oh, jah."

"Jah, sure I will." Jenny was all smiles.

As soon as the fellowship lunch was over, Emma caught up with Adam. "Our company arrived as I am sure you saw already. Want to say hello?"

Adam followed her through the crowded room. Nora and Tootie gave Adam a big hug, and Jim gave him a hearty handshake.

They moved over along the wall out of the way while men rearranged the benches.

Adam ducked his head bashfully when Nora said, "We're so glad to hear the news."

Tootie elbowed her. "We can't talk about it. Remember?"

"Sorry." Nora frowned at Tootie. "Can I at least say I'm happy to see Adam?"

"Don't see why not," Jim interrupted. "Cause I'm thinking that same thing myself."

From behind them came am excited, booming voice. "What

news do you know? What news?"

Out of the corner of her eyes, Emma saw a stout figure, dressed in black, had slipped up behind them. As heavy as Stella Strutt was, Emma couldn't figure out how she walked so quietly. Especially, when her feet were always so swelled, causing them to spilled over her black oxfords. "Stella, Mammi was talking to Adam about their visit with us." She turned to Nora. "Mammi, that is recht, ain't so?"

"Of course, that was it. Nice to see you again, Stella," Nora replied and changed the subject. "We're so glad to get to visit with everyone today that we met on our last trip to Wickenburg."

"I am glad you are having a gute time. A gute time." Stella studied them closely, obviously wondering if she'd missed something newsy they didn't want her to know.

From the kitchen doorway, Roseanna Nisely called, "Schwestern Stella, come show me where you keep this bowl?" When Stella turned her back to Emma, Roseanna had a twinkle in her light brown eyes as she winked.

Emma nodded that she understood and mouthed denki.

Nora patted Adam's arm. "Tootie and I better get into the kitchen to see if we can help with cleanup. We will talk to you again soon. Come see us as often as you can."

Adam nodded and smiled.

When Nora and Tootie disappeared through the kitchen door, Emma lamented softly, "Adam, I want to add I would like you to come see me as often as you can. It has been a long two weeks for me without seeing you."

Adam nodded agreement as he patted his chest and pointed at her.

A smile kindled in Emma's eyes. "Are you interested in a walk with me on this fine day?"

Adam flashed a smile that danced up to his eyes as he followed her out of the house.

Emma clasped her hands behind her back while they walked down the driveway. "I hoped sometime this last week you would come visit my gross eldra and aendi and me."

Adam wrote on his notepad. "Sorry. Swamped with work."

Emma teased, "That so? I worried you were trying to put off getting close to Aendi Tootie."

He grinned and scribbled,"I am up early. Making an order of furniture for a new house in the mornings, and work at the Weber sisters in the afternoons. By night, I am too tired to visit."

"What are you building for the Weber sisters?"

"A kitchen."

Emma frowned. "Ach! They are remodeling their kitchen recht now. I hope you get the job done in time for them to bake my wedding cake."

"I am not remodeling the old kitchen. I am building a new kitchen," he wrote.

Emma's eyes widened in concern. "Now of all times. What's wrong with the one they have always used?"

Adam rolled his eyes toward the sky.

"That is not gute news. They might not be able to take baking orders or serve meals for some time," Emma worried.

Adam wrote, "They will. They still have the old kitchen to cook in."

Emma was confused. "You lost me."

"When I get done, they will have two kitchens."

"Why?"

Adam shrugged.

Emma opened her mouth to ask another question. She lost her train of thought as she watched a new family walking toward their buggy. A thin woman in a faded blue dress and three skinny boys, wearing patched trousers, followed a lanky, weathered man. Each of the boys was a head taller than the next one. "Wonder where they live? This is the first time I noticed them in church."

Adam wrote, "They just moved in. My neighbors." He poked her arm to get her to look at the note.

"Neighbors. Where?"

At the old compound," Adam wrote.

Emma felt fearful at the mention of that compound, and the

Hostellers that once terrorized the neighborhood. Her hand flew to the lump forming in her throat. "They are not part of the Hosteller family, are they?"

Adam shrugged.

"They should have stayed to join in the fellowship. That is the best way to get to know all of us," Emma criticized. Under her breath, she added, "And for us to find out more about them."

Adam nodded in agreement.

"We do not want Hostellers to move in and take over again. Come with me. We need to talk to Daed and the bishop. Maybe they know something about that family." Emma grabbed Adam's hand and headed for the house.

A group of men, John Lapp and Bishop Elton Bontrager among them, were at the screen door as Emma opened it. "Coming out on the porch?" Emma backed up. As soon as the screen door shut, she said, "Adam and I are wondering if any of you talked to the new family that was at the service?"

"I greeted them when they first arrived, but they just nodded and moved away," John Lapp said.

"Anyone else talk to them?" Fear dropped from Emma's throat and tighten her chest, making it hard to breathe.

Bishop Bontrager asked, "Emma, what is this all about?"

"Adam just told me the family is living at the Hosteller compound. I am worried they might be Hostellers. Nah, I am not just worried I am scared to death."

Hamish Manwiller spoke up sharply. "We went through too much at the hands of the Hostellers to wilcom them back again. If that is who they are, I want them out of this neighborhood."

The rest of the men nodded their heads, and a few uttered soft jahs.

"Now just a minute," Elton said. "We do not know anything about these people yet. They might be innocent of what you are thinking. Remember judge not lest ye be judged. Maybe the women know something if the wife talked to them while she helped in the kitchen. I will ask. Wait here."

John patted Emma on the shoulder. "Elton's recht. Best not

get worked up until we have some answers."

Bishop Bontrager came back with Margaret Yoder, Preacher Luke Yoder's mother. He swiped the sweat on his red face with his white hanky as he said, "Schwestern Margaret says the wife helped her with the table settings."

The chunky, elderly woman folded her arms and rested them across her chest. Her brown eyes grew serious as she noted the concerned looks. "What is this about?"

"We did not get a chance to find out about the new family," Elton said. "Adam says they live on the Hosteller farm."

"Jah, Ada Jostle told me that while we worked."

"Are they kin to the Hostellers?" Hamish Manwiller demanded.

"I do not think so," Margaret said uncertainly. "Their last name is different."

"That does not mean a thing," Hamish declared.

"Hamish is right," Moses Strutt said. "The woman might be a Hosteller kin."

"They might have changed their last name so we would not know they are Hostellers," Preacher Luke Yoder suggested.

"I hear too much guessing. You cannot go off half cocked. We should wilcom the family to the community and find out more about them," Elton said.

Deacon Enos Yutzy shook his head. "Now, Bishop, how are we going to do that if they do not talk to us. I greeted the man when he sat on the end of the bench for the service and introduced myself. He said his name was Jake Jostle. That was all he said. I noticed during the service he looked down at his hands most of the time."

Abram Beiler's frizzy, gray beard moved up and down as he shook his head. "I agree. The man did not want to get acquainted when I greeted him."

Bishop Bontrager held up his hand. "Come morning, a committee of us will go visit the Jostles and make them wilcom. If we take the first step, that might make them feel more like talking."

"That sounds like a gute idea," Preacher Luke Yoder nodded

his blond head in agreement.

"Meet at my house around ten," the bishop told them. "Now we are here to spend this afternoon in fellowship. We should do just that. Bruder Abram Beiler, wie bischt du this fine Sunday?"

Abram rubbed his beard as he spoke in a slow drawl, "Ach, Bishop, I am slow in all things and getting slower by the minute."

That brought a laugh from the other men.

Elton quipped, "Praise the Lord! I know how you feel, Abram. Anymore, it is harder to tell which one is faster, me or the box turtle in my yard."

Emma whispered in Adam's ear. "You are the one I want to have fellowship with. Let's take that walk you promised me."

They walked away from the house toward a dense windbreak of tall evergreens. Once they were behind the trees, Adam wrapped his arm around Emma's waist and squeezed her side.

His warm smile and adoring eyes caused Emma to answer, "I am glad to hear that, Adam Keim."

Adam raised his eyebrows and widened his eyes, teasing her to explain.

"It is gute to hear that you love me."

Adam's smile widened as he nodded yes.

That evening, Adam and Emma went back to the Strutt farm for the singing. On the way home after the singing, Emma said, "This morning, I asked Katie Yost and Jennie Yoder to be my newehockers. Have you decided who you want for newehockers?"

Adam handed her the lines and wrote, "I asked Levi Yoder and Noah."

Emma held the paper in close to her face to make it out. She squeezed Adam's arm. "Ach, that is perfect. Katie and Levi are dating. Noah would like to take Jennie out, and she is wanting to date someone. This makes a good excuse for them to get together. You could not have made better picks."

Adam patted his shoulder, boasting about his good idea.

"Take it easy. Only my rooster, Abraham, is allowed to crow," Emma scolded playfully and handed him back the lines.

Soon they were at the Lapp farm driveway. Adam pulled back on the lines to stop Sophie when the buggy was even with the Lapp house.

Emma asked, "Will you have time to visit my grandparents and Aendi Tootie this week? They are wishing you can come for supper soon."

Adam wavered his hand back and forth.

"This week is going to be busy, too?"

Adam nodded, leaned over and kissed her cheek.

"Sure, I understand, but just remember I will miss you very much," Emma said as she climbed out of the buggy.

Adam nodded, patted his chest over his heart, snapped the lines to start his horse and left.

Emma stood on the edge of the driveway and waved at Adam until he was out of sight. If wishing made it so, they would already be married as far as she was concerned. That way Adam would be at home with her every night, and she wouldn't feel so lonely the minute he drove out of her sight.

Chapter 3

Monday near dinner time, John drove in and parked the buggy by the barn. Noah met him and started to unhitch Ben while John walked to the house.

Jim and Daniel were at the table, watching the women dish up the food.

Nora said, "Hi John, just in time for lunch."

"Gute," he said solemnly. He walked over to the wash pan and stuck his hands under the water.

At the gloomy sound in John's voice, Hal stopped placing the plates on the table to study him. "All recht, how did the visit to the Jostles go? You don't look happy."

"It did not go well. Hamish Manwiller should not have gone with us. He is still upset about what the Hostellers did to him and Edna. Our feet barely hit the ground before Hamish was in the front of the wilcom committee. Jake came down from his ladder to meet us. He is remodeling the little hog house beside the driveway so his wife can use it for a chicken house."

When John paused to dry his hands, Emma urged, "Go on, Daed. Is that family related to the Hostellers?"

"Nah, they are not. Elton shook hands with the man. He told Jake Jostle we were there to wilcom him and his family to the community. Luke Yoder said we were pleased to see him and his family in church and wanted them to continue attending.

Enos Yutzy said a new family is always a wilcom addition to

26

the community. Jake seemed to be warming up to us until Hamish butted in. He blurted out the only reason he came along was to find out if they were kin to the Hostellers."

"Ach, that's too bad," Hal said.

"Sure was. Jostle's face turned red. He asked if that was the real reason we wanted to be so friendly. He said he did not have anything to hide. He heard about the Hostellers. He was told the story by the agent when he bought the farm. He was not kin to them and did not want any more to do with the likes of them than we did. If that was all we wanted to know, he had work to do. He turned his back on us and went back to hammering on the building."

"Can you blame the poor man?" Tootie asked, tisking.

"Nah, I cannot. I am afraid we are going to have trouble now convincing him that his family is wilcom in this community," John said, plopping down at the end of the table. "After he opened his mouth, Hamish hated that he upset Jake by sounding so hostile, but too late now. The damage is done.

Emma's expression was troubled. "Now we know that family is not here to cause us trouble. We should try extra hard to convince them we want to be friends."

The next Sunday evening, Adam came to take Emma to the singing at Abram Beiler's farm. The late afternoon sunlight painted the countryside with pinks and grays.

Adam noticed Emma was too quiet. He elbowed her and pointed to the sky.

"I see it. Very pretty."

Adam was perplexed when Emma didn't add more. He elbowed her again and wavered his hand in a question.

Emma said, "I am sorry. Did you hear what happened when the wilcoming committee went to the Hosteller compound?"

Adam nodded yes.

"Hamish Manwiller really messed up the wilcom the men planned. My thoughts are with the Jostle family. I feel so bad for that new family. I wish I had not been so quick to start everyone wondering about them. We need to find a way to show them we are not as unfriendly as Hamish Manwiller made us seem."

Adam gave Sophie her head and wrote, "That family does not help make friends. They haven't shown interest in getting to know anyone. That standoffish attitude is still there."

"Ach, that is too bad, but can you blame them? Has something else happen?"

Adam wrote, "Luke Yoder took his family to visit. Linda gave Ada Jostle baked goods as a wilcom."

"That is gute. If they like any family it will be the Yoders. They are the nicest people around," Emma said.

Adam wrote, "Jake said he was too busy to talk. He needed to work on the machine shed. His wife appreciated Margaret and Linda's visit, but she is real standoffish. Mark tried to talk to the boys. They stuck their hands in their pockets and stared at their dirty feet. They nodded, but it was as if Jake had told his family not to talk to anyone. Luke said he did not have a reason to go back unless they invited him."

Emma watched the road as she sighed. "Maybe they need more time to get acquainted with everyone, besides Hamish Manwiller that is. It might take awhile for them to trust us. Once they get used to us, they will see we are all recht and friendly."

Adam nodded no as he wrote, "I heard hammering. Took my hammer over to help yesterday. Jake and the boys were roofing the machine shed. Jake said was not any use wasting my time. They could get the job done just fine without me. Friendly sounding he was not so I left. Got enough work of my own to keep me busy. I will not bother Jake again."

"Ach, Adam, we cannot give up holding out a friendly hand. I feel so sorry for that family. Imagine how lonely it is for them. They are in a strange place, living among people they think are not friendly," Emma declared as Adam pulled back on the lines to stop Sophie by the other buggies.

Later that evening after she returned home from the singing, Emma followed Hal to the Lapp kitchen with empty popcorn bowls. "Adam does not think much of the new family. Yesterday, Jake Jostle was not friendly to Adam when he offered to help roof the machine shed. The family did not warm up to the Yoders, either. I want to introduced myself as the teacher. I certainly do not want the boys afraid to go to school this fall. It might help if they get to know me before school starts."

"Sounds like a gute idea to me," Hal agreed. "The family need to know I'm the nurse in the area. They left so soon after dinner last Sunday I didn't get a chance to talk to them."

"But … ." Emma paused as she stacked the bowls in the dishpan.

"What's the problem?"

"I am hesitant to go back to the compound. It is such a scary place for me. I have nothing but bad memories of that farm."

"There's not anyone there to harm you now." That didn't comfort Emma. "How about I go with you so I can introduce myself? That way if they need any medical help they will know where to come."

Emma brightened up considerably. "Ach, denki, Hallie. I would feel so much better if you went with me."

"We could take them a wilcom to the neighborhood offering. How about a loaf of bread and a jar of your blackberry jam."

"All recht, but Adam said the Yoders took a wilcom basket already. They didn't think Jake was impressed. He does not care now if his neighbors are trying to be friendly," Emma said.

"Can you blame Jake after the way Hamish sounded so unfriendly?"

"Nah, I cannot. That is why we should not give up for the sake of Ada and the boys. I wish that family could see we are all not like Hamish Manwiller," Emma insisted.

"All we can do is keep trying and hope they decide to turn the other cheek," Hal said.

The next morning, Hal and Emma left Nora and Tootie cutting material into pieces for a quilt. They wanted to make it for Emma and Adam as a wedding gift.

Nora said she was glad Hal and Emma had some place to go for awhile. She didn't want two Amish women watching Tootie and her cut and sew quilt pieces. Tootie agreed that would make her very nervous.

As Hal and Emma went out the door, Tootie said, "I want to cut out the squares."

"Why?" Nora asked.

"They're easier than triangles," Tootie said truthfully.

"So? All the pieces need to be cut out." Tootie's lower lip push out in a pout. Nora gave in. "All right, just start cutting, but the squares are small. I don't see how they could be easier than the triangles."

On the porch, Hal whispered, "Suppose it's safe to leave them alone while we're gone?"

Emma smiled. "I think their bickering is in fun." With a sideways glance at Hal, she added softly, "Most of the time."

That remark made them giggle.

As Hal turned the buggy onto the driveway at the Jostle farm, they noticed the buildings looked worse than they remembered.

"It doesn't take long for buildings to run down when no one is using them, ain't so?" Hal commented.

Emma exclaimed, "Jah, but see how good the hen house looks and the machine shed. Jake has made a difference already on this farm. Look back of the house at that large garden."

"Jah," Hal said. "Plants are up enough to row them. Ada has a nice garden already."

Jake and his boys were by the barn. Jake hammered a board over a hole in the wall. The smallest boy followed his father. He struggled to hold up a heavy bucket of nails high enough that it didn't drag on the ground. The middle boy carried a rotten board over to a pile of scraps. The oldest boy swung a hand scythe, cutting dry weeds along the building's foundation. The wooden handle was longer than he was tall.

They stopped what they were doing to stare at the buggy coming toward them. Emma and Hal climbed down and walked to the edge of the barn yard. They stopped just short of the head high iron weeds and knee high lambquarters patches.

"Gute morning," Hal greeted.

Jake nodded in her direction.

30

"I am Hallie Lapp, and this is my daughter, Emma. We noticed you at the worship service and want to wilcom you to the community."

"Ach, des gute," Jake snorted. His thick lips pushed a curved line through his bushy beard that said otherwise.

Emma focused on the boys. "I am the teacher. I look forward to seeing you boys in school this fall. What are your names?"

The boys looked at each other and at their father. Jake nodded at them. The oldest boy said sullenly, "My name is Albert. I am done with school."

"And your name?" Emma asked the middle boy.

His face reddened as he stared at his bare feet. "I am Sam."

The youngest of the three eyed her and chirped, "Will."

"It is nice to meet all of you," Emma said.

Hal added, "I'm the nurse for this area. My clinic is built onto our house. If you need medical help, we don't live very far from here."

"I know where you live," Jake said curtly, staring at the hammer in his hands.

Emma looked around. "You are certainly making an improvement on these old buildings. It will be nice to drive by here and see the barn yard filled with animals. Do you have chickens for the hen house yet?"

"Nah," Jake uttered, eying the hole filled barn roof as if he'd like to get started on it.

"The Wickenburg Salebarn has a small animal sale on Wednesday. That is a gute place to buy chickens and rabbits among other things. That is where I get my chickens," Emma offered.

"You are busy. We don't want to interrupt any longer. Would it be all recht if we visit with your wife a few minutes?" Jake had a hard expression on his face. He probably suspected their visit with his wife wouldn't be friendly. "Just to say hello," Hal added.

"Jah," he answered begrudgingly.

"We will leave you to your work." Hal turned toward the house.

Emma retrieved the food basket from the buggy as Hal knocked on the front door. Ada Jostle appeared at the screen door, wiping her hands on her apron. In a squeaky voice that sounded like two tree limbs rubbing together in a high wind, she asked, "Jah, what is it?"

"I am Hallie Lapp. This is my daughter, Emma. We just dropped by to wilcom you and your family to the community. Might we visit a moment?"

Ada's thin face showed her weary interest as she eyed the women. She opened the door for them. "Jah, wilcom."

Hal handed her the basket. "We brought you a wilcom gift."

"Denki, come in," Ada said.

Hal and Emma stood just inside the door. It took a minute for their eyes to adjust to coming out of the sunlight into the dim house.

Ada released a nervous cough as she pointed to the three chairs near the heating stove. "Would you like to sit down?"

"Denki, we won't stay long. You must be busy," Hal said, sitting in one of the chairs. "I want to tell you I'm the nurse for the community. I have a clinic on the side of my house at the Lapp farm. If you need medical help or birthing needs, you can come see me or send a member of the family to get me to come to you."

"Des gute to know," Ada said earnestly as she slipped onto a chair.

"I am the teacher. I look forward to your sons attending school this fall," Emma told her, standing beside Hal.

Ada gathered her apron in her hands restlessly. "Denki. Albert is out of school."

"That is what he told me," Emma replied.

An awkward silence fell over the room. It was clear Ada was not used to company or making small talk with women. Finally, Hal tried again. "We'll be having a quilting frolic soon. I can let you know when. That's a gute way to get acquainted with other women in the neighborhood."

Ada looked uncomfortable about the invitation, but she said politely, "Sure."

Hal said to Emma, "Perhaps, we should go now." She turned to Ada. "It's been nice talking to you. We'll see you and your family at the next worship service Sunday next."

"I hope so," Ada said in almost a whisper as she stared out the window toward the barn.

As Emma drove away, she sounded discouraged, "That visit did not go well."

"At least we tried. This is not all our fault. Something happened to make that family distrust people, and whatever it was took place long before they moved here."

"I told you this place gives me a bad feeling. That same feeling may have rubbed off on that poor family since they moved in," Emma said.

"Surely you don't believe that can happen," Hal scolded. "Living here wouldn't instill distrust in them. Just in case though, when people grumble about that family, we need to remind everyone the Jostles aren't to blame for what happened at the compound. Did you notice how frazzled Ada appeared?"

"Jah, that poor soul is worn out."

"I'm sure she works hard, but worry can be a big part of the way she feels," Hal said.

The next morning during kitchen cleanup, Hal announced after dinner, she'd take the women over to visit the Weber sisters. Emma wanted to talk to them about baking the wedding cake. While she scraped a plate over the scrap pail, Emma frowned at the suggestion.

"What? Aren't you ready to set up the date with the sisters so they will be prepared to bake your cake? It takes a lot of ingredients for a four layer cake."

"Ach jah, I know, but Adam told me news after the Sunday service that bothered me. He is working for the sisters. He is building a new kitchen. Adam says something odd is going on over there, but he has not figured out what it is yet," Emma shared.

"We best find out recht away. I don't mind baking sheet cakes, but I don't want the task of the fancy wedding cake," Hal assured her. "If the sisters can't bake the cake, we need to find someone else to help us recht away."

That afternoon, Hal hitched up the enclosed buggy. She walked back to the house and stuck her head around the screen door. "Are all of you ready?"

Tootie gripped her sister's arm. "I think you, and I should stay home, Nora."

"Whatever for. I want to go," Nora declared.

Hal stepped inside. "Why don't you want to come with us, Aunt Tootie?"

"We can watch the little girls for you while you're gone," Tootie offered.

"No need to worry. Daniel is going to stay here while they nap. Besides, we won't be gone long."

"Well... well, your mother and I really do need to finish Emma's quilt top."

"Tootie! We only have one row of blocks left. I can sew that much this evening after supper," Nora scolded. "We're going to visit the Weber sisters." She pointed a stiff finger toward outside. "Go!"

Tootie pushed her lower lip out, pouting in surrender, but she climbed into the buggy with the others.

Just before Hal drove through the branch, they passed an open buggy driven by a woman. Her passenger was a small girl, smiling as if she was having a good time. Nora said, "Isn't that the cutest little girl? Look at her, Tootie?"

"She is that," Tootie said shortly.

"That little girl is *enjoying* her ride. I wonder if the woman is her grandma?" Nora put an emphases on enjoying.

Tootie gave a soft harrumph.

"Hal, that's the first buggy I've noticed that has fenders over the wheels," Nora said.

"Since I've lived in this area, I've seen several changes in buggies that's for sure," Hal told her.

From the back, Emma added, "The fenders keep rocks from flying on people and helps with dust control."

"We're here, Aunt Tootie," Hal said over her shoulder as she turned into the Weber driveway.

"They certainly have a big enough mailbox," Tootie observed, looking out the back window.

"Read the sign under it," Nora pointed out. "All Things Are Open To The Lord."

Hal stopped the buggy in front of the Weber sisters large farm house. Three horses stopped grazing, trotted to the barn yard fence and whinnied at the visitors. Two were large blond draft horses, and the other one was a dark red horse.

After they climbed out of the buggy, Tootie eyed the horses. Emma told her, "The two work horses are Adam's. He uses them to pull his carpenter wagon. The other one belongs to the Weber sisters. They use that one to pull their buggy."

Adam's large, carpenter wagon held his tools and work order supplies. It was parked along side the house in the shade while Bobby and Adam worked in the house.

The Weber sisters came out on the porch to greet them.

"Wilcom," greeted Eve, the tall, thin talkative sister.

Short, heavy set, Esther, a woman of few words, nodded and smiled her greeting.

"My parents and aunt are visiting with us. This is Nora Lindstrom and Tootie Klinefeld," Hal introduced.

"Come inside," Eve said.

When the women entered the kitchen, hammers pounded in rhythm in the next room.

"What is going on in there?" Hal asked in a loud voice as if she hadn't heard the remodeling news from Emma.

Esther folded her arms and rested them in front of her apron as she looked at the floor.

Eve replied, "My new kitchen. I can hardly wait to cook in it when the Keim brothers get it built."

"Oh," Hal said quietly. Esther didn't look one bit pleased to share this news of two kitchens. It was a good time to change the subject. Though as she looked at the counters filled with breads, rolls and desserts, Hal decided this one kitchen had been plenty productive so far for the two sisters.

Eve said, "It has been awhile since we had a chance to visit. It's so gute to see both of you and your company. Sorry for all the noise, but it cannot be helped." She pointed toward the table." Do sit down, ladies, so we can visit. Schwestern, serve our guests a cup of hot tea. I will dish up the sticky buns."

Esther nodded as she rushed to the stove. She picked up the steaming tea kettle and poured hot water through a strainer, filled with tea leaves, she held over a pan.

Eve scooped six sticky pecan buns onto saucers and put one in front of each guest and two other places for Esther and her. When she stopped by Emma, she clasped her hands together. "We have been expecting you. We hear you are getting married to one of those young carpenters in the next room. He told us so."

"Adam told you?"

Eve grinned. "Jah, only because he knew we were going to find out soon when you came to make arrangements for the wedding cake. That is why you are here, ain't so?"

Emma simply said, "Jah."

As she poured the hot tea into a row of cups, Esther added, "Good choice of husbands, Emma. Jesus was a carpenter." She set each cup on a saucer. "Now, Schwestern, help me serve."

"Sure!" Eve said curtly as she rushed to get two cups.

"While the tea cools, I am going to say gute morning to Adam and Bobby," Emma said, heading for the next room.

She didn't stay gone too long.

"That was quick," Tootie said when Emma slipped into the chair next to her.

"I did not want my tea to get cold, and the men are too busy to talk," Emma said.

When the cups went empty, Esther asked, "Would anyone like to see our garden? It is doing as gute as it can this summer."

"I would," Emma said enthusiastically. "I always learn something that helps me garden when I look at your garden."

"I believe I will stay here and visit with Eve about the wedding," Hal said. "The rest of you go."

Wishing she could listen to the wedding talk instead, Tootie huffed a protest under her breath at being included. She didn't want to look at another garden. She couldn't think of a way out of the garden tour so she followed the others out the door. The garden was important to the Weber sisters, and Tootie didn't want to hurt their feelings.

Hal decided Adam was right. Odd things were happening at the Weber house. "Esther usually lets you show everyone the garden. This is a switch."

Eve released a gusty sigh as she looked toward the closed door of her soon to be new kitchen. "There is soon to be more switches. A lot is the matter in this house, and it has been that way a gute long time. After all these years, Esther and I still cannot agree on how to cook in this kitchen or plant a garden."

"That is hard for me to believe. You both do such a wonderful job at everything you do. As for cooking, your food is always delicious," declared Hal.

"We have always tried to please our customers, but it has not been without disagreements between us. I guess I am not handling how I disagree with Esther as well as I once did. I do not give in as easily as before. Maybe it is I am older and less patient, ain't so?" Eve rubbed her forehead as if thinking about her problems gave her a headache.

"I don't know about that," Hal said diplomatically. She didn't want to appear to take sides between these two nice women, but she could sympathize completely. She didn't feel old, and she certainly had trouble being patient with Tootie sometimes.

"Jah, you would not yet. Just wait a few years. You will understand better this conversation after you have grown older," Eve predicted.

"If you don't mind me asking, what do Esther and you disagree about?"

"Eve stood up and pointed to a pot on the back of the cook stove. "The kettle simmering is beef stew to feed the carpenters for dinner and supper. After it simmered an hour this morning, I sampled the stew. I said it tasted just recht."

"After all these years, I'm sure we all trust your judgment," Hal empathized.

"You might, but Esther tasted the stew and told me it needed more salt. I told her it was salty enough. She poured a tablespoon full in the kettle too quick for me to stop her. A whole tablespoon of salt mind you. Now I fear the stew is ruined. The Keim brothers will not like it."

"I see." Hal stared at the large kettle, wondering how much salt was too much for a pan that size as she searched for words of comfort. She certainly wasn't the right person to talk to if Eve wanted a good cook to side with her. "Well, I wouldn't worry. The men will be so hungry after working all day. They will eat anything."

"Ach! It looks like they will have to, ain't so? The damage is already done. They have no choice," Eve moaned, stuffing her hands in her apron pockets.

"Does this disagreement in seasoning have something to do with why you're building the new kitchen?"

"Jah, I cannot keep criticizing my schwestern when she will not listen to me. I do not want to always feel bad for the diners when the food does not taste recht. We will have two menus when the new kitchen is finished. Diners can choose to eat my meal or Esther's."

"Looks like you solved the problem like Solomon by cutting the baby in half," Hal offered cryptically.

Eve opened her mouth to respond but didn't when she heard the hollow sound of sensible shoes on the board porch floor.

Emma was the first one in the door. She seemed concerned about something. "Hallie, you *really do need* to go look at the garden. It is so neat. Not a weed in it."

Hal assumed that meant Emma listened to the other sister's version of the disagreement. Nora came in behind Emma, and she nodded her head in agreement with Emma. Hal didn't know what she could do to help, but listening didn't hurt anything. "All recht! Esther, you show me the garden while Emma discusses with Eve how she wants her wedding cake decorated."

"Jah," Esther said.

Tootie asked, "Did I miss a good discussion about the wedding, Hallie?"

Hal gave Emma an disquieting glance. "Nah, Aunt Tootie, we didn't get around to it so you didn't miss a thing. Now you can listen while Emma tells Eve about the wedding."

As Hal and Esther went out the door, Emma said, "Can you make honeysuckle flowers from icing? I would like honeysuckles on my wedding cake."

Hal walked beside Esther on the sidewalk to the garden gate in silence which is what Hal expected. Esther didn't talk much. Hal learned some time ago to give up on providing a running conversation with Esther and just enjoy the mutual silence.

Hal looked across the garden and exclaimed, "Emma is right. Eve and you have a lovely garden this time."

The elderly woman looked up at her with a weak smile.

Hal pointed across the rows. "What's that staked string for through the middle?"

"That divides the garden in half. The half nearest us is mine, and the other half is Schwestern's," Esther said quietly.

"Oh," Hal uttered. "I never knew you to divide the garden before."

"Ach! We never did. We always planted according to the Amish rule of thumb and our faith in our beliefs."

"What is that?" Hal asked.

Esther recited, "First, plant five rows of peas: preparedness, promptness, perseverance, politeness, and prayer. Next, plant three rows of squash: squash gossip, squash criticism, squash indifference. Two rows of turnips: Turn up with a smile. Turn up with determination. Finally, five rows of lettuce. Let us be faithful. Let us be unselfish. Let us be loyal. Let us be truthful. Let us love one another. After that, we plant the rest of the garden in other vegetables."

"I see the rows you're talking about minus the peas. Of course, those are finished by now," Hal said.

"Jah, I sewed turnip seeds in those rows, and that has not come up yet. We look forward to that crop. The tops make gute greens while the turnips grow."

"But why did you divide the garden in half?" Hal pressed.

"Schwestern wanted to plant too many vegetables I did not

want in the garden. We need more vegetables, we can cook and can, to use for our diners and for our winter use. I could not talk her out of planting her way so I divided the garden."

Hal said, "I see." Esther just spoke more words in this conversation than Hal had ever heard from her before.

"Ach! My sister is not very practical in her old age and very stubborn as well," Esther said peevishly.

Hal didn't understand. "What's wrong with the vegetables on Eve's end of the garden?"

"Broccoli and cauliflower for one thing," Esther said peevishly.

"Those are gute, healthy vegetables, ain't so?"

"They are, but the plants are large. They take a lot of room for vegetables that makes one head and is done. They do not produce enough food," Esther complained.

"Ach, I see," Hal said. She didn't know how to dispute that claim. She wasn't any better gardener than she was a cook, and she didn't want to appear to take sides. The garden and the kitchen were disagreements the sisters would have to work out by themselves. "The large yellow marigolds scattered among the vegetables are certainly pretty."

"Jah, the flowers are doing a gute job of insect control this year," Esther said, sounding upbeat when she delivered that news.

On the way home, Hal asked, "Emma, do you know the Amish rule of thumb for planting a garden that Esther told me about?"

"Jah, but we do not need so many rows of some of the vegetables so I cannot go by it. It is different for the Weber sisters. They use so much of what the garden produces in their business. Still, it was strange to see a string dividing the garden."

"Did Esther tell you why the string is there?" Hal asked.

"Jah," Emma said quietly.

"I'm worried about the Weber sisters. I've never seen them at such odds before. Imagine, their situation is so bad Eve is spending a lot of money to build an extra kitchen."

"I can see why," Tootie said. "Asking two women that are sisters to share a kitchen peaceably is like throwing two wet cats in a sack and tying it shut. It's bad enough they have to share a home."

"Sage advice from your Aunt Tootie," Nora cracked.

Chapter 4

The next morning, two hours before daylight, John slipped out of bed and dressed. He tapped on the spare room door to wake Jim and on the boys door to wake them.

It wasn't long until they gathered in the kitchen. John said, "Since we need to hurry this morning, once the chores are done we will come back in to eat breakfast."

Jim said, "Got ya."

Daniel nodded, and Noah yawned.

When they stepped outside, Jim stretched. "It's good to get an early start on the day." He laughed at the flock of crows that shattered the silence, themselves startled by such an early commotion. His laughter woke up Abraham. "The rooster heard me and thinks he overslept this morning."

"Jah," John agreed. "But ain't it nice to get up early enough to watch Mother Nature wake up the day." He pointed to the pink sky in the eastern horizon.

"Sure is. Nothing nicer than listening to the proud morning crow of a rooster, and birds chirping wake up calls in the trees," Jim said.

"Jah, and with a long work day ahead of us, it is gute we got a gute night's sleep. Ich hab wie ein murmeltier gepennt."

Jim grinned. "Slow down and come again with that one."

"I said I slept like a ground hog," John explained.

"Me, too. Only I slept like a log," Jim replied.

Once they entered the barn, everyone swung into action. Jim opened the back door to let in the first six Holsteins. The large black and white cows plodded to their stalls. Eager to be fed and milked, they shifted their feet impatiently while they waited.

Daniel dumped feed in front of each cow, and Noah sanitized the cow bags.

John turned on the generator and followed behind Noah. He spoke softly to each cow to get her attention so she'd stand quietly as he attached the milkers.

While they waited to release the cows, John joined Jim, Noah and Daniel and leaned against the wall. "Remember, boys, not a word about what we are really doing today."

Noah nodded."

Daniel said, "I know."

Jim patted Daniel on the shoulder. "Good boys."

After breakfast, Hal told Nora and Tootie, "We're free today while our men and boys help Samuel Nicely make his hay. How about a shopping trip this morning and lunch out with my friend, Barb Sloan, from the Home Health Agency? Emma wants to invite her to the wedding.

First, we'll go to the fabric shop. We need to buy the material for Emma's wedding dress and her attendants' dresses. It's time they get their sewing done."

Tootie leaned closer to Nora and whispered, "Another buggy ride. Why can't we take your car?"

"We can," Nora said softly. "Hallie, we can use my car. I'd be glad to drive. It would be faster if you have much shopping to do for the wedding."

"That is a great idea, Mom," Hal said.

"It wasn't her idea. It was mine," Tootie put in quickly.

"She's right. It was Tootie's idea," Nora agreed.

"Thank you, Aunt Tootie for thinking of it, and thank you, Mom, for driving your car."

"I thought it was a good idea," Tootie boasted. "If we have time, could we stop by a store that sells bouquets of silk flowers?"

Nora asked, "Why do you need flowers?"

"I want to put them on Peter Rogies's grave while we're here," Tootie said quietly.

"For that, we'll make time," Hal said as she hugged Tootie."

Once they reached Wickenburg, Nora parked in front of the Home Health Agency office. Hal's friend and former boss stared at her over papers in her hands as Hal walked toward her. "Hello, Barb."

"Hello right back at you, Girlfriend." She stretched her neck to look out the window. "Hey, did you just get out of that car?" You give up being Amish?"

"No, not now, not ever. I don't want to leave my family."

Barb wrinkled her nose at Hal. "And here I was hoping you might want your old job back. You can start tomorrow."

Hal laughed. "Don't you wish! Will you stop talking and give me a minute to explain my visit? My parents and aunt are visiting. My mother drove us in to shop. It's a ladies day out, and we wondered if you'd like to eat lunch with us."

"Sure, where?"

"How about the Maidrite. The meal is on me," Hal said.

"Can't beat a free lunch. A maidrite sounds better than the peanut butter sandwich and chips in my sack lunch. Noon all right?"

"That should work fine. We'll get the shopping out of the way in Bloomfield, and I want to show my relatives around Wickenburg before lunch." Hal hurried to the door. "See you later."

The women spent a couple of hours in the fabric shop at Bloomfield, picking out material. Enough for three dresses in periwinkle blue and thread to match. White organdy for three aprons and two white prayer caps for the attendants. Enough black organdy to make Emma a wedding prayer cap and another one as a spare.

Next stop was The Maidrite. The cafe was always busy at lunch time. Hal looked across the room and spotted an empty table large enough for all of them. She led the way.

Owner of the Maidrite, Susie Davidson, blond hair plastered

under a hairnet, came to the table. She pulled a pen from over her ear and poised her pad. "Hey, nice to see you, Hal and Emma. Been awhile."

"It has, indeed," Hal replied. "Meet my mother, Nora Lindstrom and my Aunt Tootie Klinefeld."

"Nice to meet you, ladies. Welcome to Wickenburg. What can I bring you guys for lunch?"

"The maidrites, of course, with salads and iced tea," Hal said. "And put this all on one tab. I'm buying."

Barb walked up behind Susie and slid into the empty chair. "Want one more meal to add to your list?"

Susie smiled."That's fine with me, Barb. One more customer is always what we want around here."

"How's that brother of yours?" Barb asked. "I never see him around town anymore."

"Bud stays pretty close to home now that he and Elizabeth are married. Latest news is, we're expecting a new addition to the family," Susie said, beaming.

"Congratulations," Tootie said. "When are you due?"

Susie giggled. "Oh no, not me. My brother and his wife are having the baby. I'm just going to be the aunt."

"That's such wonderful news. Always a thrill to have a new baby in the family," Hal said.

"Take it from me, Susie, aunts are good to have around, too," Tootie retorted.

"Speaking for us aunts everywhere, I completely agree. Thanks for saying that, Tootie. Now I best get busy on your orders so you can eat."

After Susie left for the kitchen, Hal said, "Barb, Emma has some news for you."

"What's up, Emma?"

Blushing as she ducked her head, Emma said softly, "I am getting married in September."

"That's wonderful. Who is the lucky fellow as if I don't already know?"

"Adam Keim."

"Un huh," Barb answered knowingly.

45

"We wondered if you might like to come to the wedding and celebrate the day with us?" Hal invited.

"I'd love to," Barb accepted.

After lunch and a trip to the Walmart so Tootie could buy a large bouquet of silk, white lilies, Nora drove them home. That evening, Emma spent a couple hours at the treadle sewing machine, sewing on her dress. In three days, she had the blue dress, cape and organdy apron done.

One afternoon, Emma hitched up the buggy and drove over to the former schoolteacher's house to ask her to be the substitute teacher during September. After Ellen Yost and Andy Miller married, they moved into a house down the road from the Yost farm. Andy worked for Ellen's father as a farm hand.

Emma picked up her teacher ledgers from the seat and descended from the buggy. Ellen opened the door. Emma was surprised to see the fair haired woman had a bulging stomach and a slight waddle as she led the way to the kitchen. "Sit down. I have a fresh pitcher of ice tea made. Help yourself to an oatmeal cookie?"

Emma reached for a cookie. "Sure is hot out, ain't so?"

"Jah. Reckon we will be glad to see fall," Ellen agreed, pouring the tea.

Emma thought back. It did not seem so long since she'd talked to Ellen, but it must have been longer than she realized. She bit into her oatmeal cookie and watched the little girl, close to two years old, the image of her mother, stack blocks on the floor. From the look of Ellen's middle, it appeared she was due to deliver another baby soon.

"The cookie is gute," Emma complimented as Ellen set the frosted glasses on the table. She washed the cookie down with a drink of tea. "You make the best mint tea."

"It's because of the gute crop of mint this year," Ellen said humbly.

Emma took another drink and swallowed slowly. "Spearmint or peppermint? I cannot tell, but the flavor is so refreshing."

Ellen slid into her chair and took a sip of tea from her frosted glass. "Spearmint. I am not fond of the taste of peppermint leaves. How are your wedding plans coming?"

"You heard already," Emma gasped.

"Jah, Katie could not wait to come visit after she talked to you. She was eager to tell me she was one of your attendants," Emma said, smiling.

"Hallie and I are working on the details. Hallie's folks and aendi have come to help. The deacon will publish our announcement at the first worship service in September. I am looking for a substitute teacher to start school for me until after the wedding. I had thought to ask you to help me, but I am not sure you will be able to help me."

"I am not as far along as I look. The reason my waist is expanding so quickly is Doctor Burns thinks I am having twins," Ellen shared bashfully.

"Really! Are you going to deliver at the hospital instead of the clinic then?"

"Jah, that will be safer for the babies. I should be able to teach through September as long as I can bring Sara with me. I am not due until the middle of October."

"Denki for offering, but I think you are going to have you hands full with Sara while you wait to deliver. So much you will have to do to get ready for twins. I will find someone else to teach."

"I feel fine. Just moving a little slower, and standing up from a chair is harder as the time goes by," Ellen said with a giggle.

"I can understand that. You need to take care of yourself and get as much rest as you can," Emma said.

While Emma peeled potatoes for supper, her mind wandered to Ellen's struggle to get up from the chair to walk to the door with her. No telling how awkward getting around was going to be for the poor woman by September. Ellen was not a good choice for teacher, but who would be?

Hal opened a jar of corn and poured the contents into a pan. "Think one jar is enough for all of us?"

Emma didn't answer.

Hal turned to the girl. Emma was staring off into space with

47

her knife poised over a potato. "Emma, was ist letz?"

Emma didn't hear her.

"Emma," Hal repeated.

"Was ist letz?" asked Emma as she started peeling again.

"Funny you should ask. I just asked you that question."

"Ach, just mulling over my visit with Ellen Miller this afternoon. You should know Ellen will not come to the clinic for her birthing in the fall."

"Is that so?"

"Jah, she is having twins, so she is going to Wickenburg to the dochtah. She wants to have the babies in the hospital."

"Gute! That eases my mind to know she'll get the care she needs. Twin births are more worry than a single. Besides, we won't have to worry about taking the birthing bed away from Aunt Tootie this time." Hal giggled, remembering the last time Tootie slept in that bed. She had to give it up in the middle of the night to Mary Mast when Mary was in labor.

Emma absentmindedly watched the road out the kitchen window. "Ellen is due in late October so Aendi Tootie would be gone by then anyway."

"But... ." Hal sensed there had to be more from the worried look on Emma's face. Emma wasn't listening to her. Hal repeated louder, "But... ."

Emma turned to face her. "Ach, I told Ellen I would find someone else to teach for the month of September. She would have tried to do it for me, but I did not want her to in her condition. Now it wonders me, who I can get to help me out?"

"Have faith. Someone will step forward to substitute teach for you. Worse come to worse, I'll volunteer," Hal said.

"You be the teacher?"

"Don't sound so surprised. I could fake it long enough to give you the time off."

"I suppose, but you have Redbird and Beth to take care of and your duties here."

"Mom and Aunt Tootie can stick around long enough to take care of the girls until September is over," Hal countered.

"Maybe, we will see," Emma said as she stared down the

road, wishing she could tell Adam about her worries.

"Now quit worrying, and tell me if I need to open up another quart of corn."

Emma didn't answer. Hal sighed, picked up the second quart jar and emptied it in the pan.

Nora and Tootie finished the purple, blue and white milky way quilt top and were anxious to get the quilting done before the wedding. At the next worship service, Hal announced she was having a quilting frolic. She told the women her mother and aunt sewed the top for Emma to put in her hope chest and would like to see it finished into a quilt.

Some women nodded knowingly and winked behind Hal's back. After all, they had seen Adam and Emma together for several years now. It wasn't too hard to figure out a wedding was in their future.

The women just didn't know when. They knew better than to ask until the couple's announcement was published with the date and invitations at a Sunday worship service.

This quilt frolic was the big neighborhood event of the month. On a Wednesday afternoon, Amish women drove in and parked their buggies in lines along the Lapp driveway. One of the later arrivals, Joe Kitzmiller stopped to drop Rachel off. The elderly woman slowly made her way to the house.

Hal and Emma greeted Rachel on the porch. "Wilcom. Come into the living room. The quilting frames are set up. Ready to go." Hal waved and shouted, "Gute morning, Joe." Joe waved as he turned his buggy around and left.

Emma said, "Your husband is in a hurry."

Rachel's wrinkled face crinkled as she grinned. "Sure. He is going to the salebarn for the day. It wonders me that this has become a very important job on Wednesdays now. When he comes back by he will stop for me."

While the women quilted, laughter and childish chatter told them their older children were having a good time, playing outside. The babies were on one quilt, and toddlers were on another in the corner of the living room where the mothers could watch them.

Mary Mast darted a glance at Hal, sitting next to her, as she pulled her thread through the layers. "What are your men doing today?"

"John took my father and the boys to the salebarn for the day. They were going to eat lunch there and make a day out of it."

"Es a voonderball gute day to be quilting, ain't so?" Edna Manwiller noted.

"Yes, nothing but mare's tail clouds in the sky. We can't ask for better weather in summer," Nora agreed.

"How is your apple crop this year?" Roseanna Nisely asked Jane Bontrager.

Jane leaned her head back and studied the light coming through the eye of her needle so she could rethread. "The trees are plenty full of apples, even though we lost a few earlier when that last wind storm went through."

Roseanna said, "I asked around, and we will all have enough apples to have an apple frolic when they ripen if everyone wants to come to our house to work the apples up."

"Count us in," Margaret Yoder said, cutting the shortened thread on top the quilt.

Stella Strutt watched Tootie's stitches as much as she did her own. Finally, she said, "I am glad to see you have improved your stitches. Improved your stitches indeed. You have I see. You have improved very much since the last time we quilted together. The last time we quilted together."

Tootie blushed. She remembered all too well sewing Stella's apron to the quilt at Jane Bontrager's quilting frolic. Stella fell on top the quilting frame when she stood up. Tootie had the feeling Stella was rubbing that day in by bringing it back to the memories of the ladies. In fact, the titters and giggles around her assured Tootie the women did remember.

A glance at Nora's stern face told Tootie she better let by gones be by gones. She smiled sweetly at Stella. "Thank you. I'm glad you approve." That must have been the right words to say. Hal winked at her.

Midday, the women stopped for a light lunch and fed the children before they went back to quilting. Later that afternoon, they finished the quilt.

Nora said, "Thank you so much, everyone. It's so good to see the quilt done. Many hands make light work."

The women said jah in union.

Hal said, "Come to the kitchen. We'll have a glass of ice tea and a piece of Emma's chocolate cake. Emma, call the children in for punch Kool aid and sugar cookies."

"Sounds gute," Roseanna said, stretching her stiff shoulders. "I am ready for a break."

Emma said, "I think the children would rather snack on the porch like a picnic."

Nora picked up the pitcher and a stack of glasses. She headed for the front porch. "I'll help serve the children."

Emma followed with a plate of cookies. Once the children were served, Emma and Nora came back. Emma sat in an empty chair between Roseanna Nisely and Margaret Yoder.

While Hal went after the cake in the pantry, Tootie got glasses and poured the tea. Hal placed a saucer of cake in front of Rachel Kitzmiller. "Have you heard that Ellen Miller is having twins?"

"Nah, I did not know. When her time comes is she coming here?"

"Nah, She told Emma she's going to Wickenburg hospital."

"Sounds like a gute idea. I know I am getting too old a midwife for a birthing with twins. Too much worry," Rachel admitted.

Hal smiled. "I know how you feel, Rachel. I was relieved when Ellen picked the hospital instead of me."

Emma stared at her saucer with a worried expression and pushed a bite of cake around with her fork.

Margaret whispered, "Emma, is something wrong?"

"Jah," Emma whispered back. "I was going to ask Ellen Miller to substitute teach for me for the month of September. I guess Jenny has mentioned why."

"Jah."

"Well, Ellen is in no shape to help me even though she was willing to give teaching a try. Now I have to find someone else, and I do not know who to ask."

Margaret leaned over to Emma's ear. "Ask me. I think it would be fun to teach for a few days."

Emma dropped her fork on her plate. "Really?"

Margaret grinned and shook her head yes.

Emma felt so much better with one of her problems solved. Now she could enjoy visiting with Roseanna Nisely. "Samuel is probably glad his hay is put up now."

Roseanna seemed very puzzled. "Samuel has not made his hay yet. It has been so dry the hay is growing slow. What made you think he made hay?"

Flustered, Emma said, "Ach, I must have heard wrong. Must be another farmer that Daed, Dawdi and the boys helped."

Why would Daed tell Hal he was going to help Samuel Nisely make hay when he didn't? The men were gone all that day. What had Daed, Dawdi and her brothers done that they didn't want the women to know about?

After Hal finished serving the cake and sat down, a cool eastern breeze blew through the kitchen window. "That sure feels gute on my hot back."

"It does indeed. Does indeed," Stella Strutt said, wiping her sweaty forehead with her paper napkin.

Hal took a bite of Emma's rich chocolate cake. As she chewed, she laid her fork on her saucer to brush a ticklish spot on her left arm. She picked up the fork, caught a small movement and thought it was a fly.

On the fork tines was a tiny brown grasshopper. It jumped and landed in the middle of her chocolate frosting and stuck there like it would on a sticky fly strip.

As the grasshopper struggled, Hal glanced around her. Thank goodness everyone was too busy eating to notice. Hal eased her fork under the insect and placed it on the side of the saucer and buried it in frosting. She laid the corner of her napkin on top of icing and continued to eat her cake. The grasshopper must have come inside earlier on Emma or her mother's clothes.

Stella laid her fork down and rubbed the back of her prayer cap. "Felt a tickle on my head. Sweating under my prayer cap, Sweating for sure."

Hal peered where Stella rubbed. Two small grasshoppers were mashed to Stella's prayer cap. A batch of the little hoppers was on Stella back, edging slowly up her shoulders, nearing Stella's neckline.

Hal's arm felt prickly. She looked down. Horrified, she found a brown line of grasshoppers parading over the roll of her long sleeve at the elbow and marching on her bare forearm toward her hand. Panic set in. Where were all these grasshoppers coming from? Hal glanced around the table. Margaret had them on her, too. In a matter of seconds, Stella realized the grasshoppers were on her when they reached her neck.

Stella, Margaret and Hal squirmed. The grasshoppers leaped and landed on the table, in the sticky saucers and dived into the ice tea. As the women on Hal's side the table gasped in unison, the women on the other side looked up to see what was wrong. Jane, Mary, Nora, Rachel and Tootie stared at the grasshoppers marching across the table toward them. Hal went into action, smashing grasshoppers with her hands. The other women slapped grasshoppers crawling near them.

Stella exclaimed in a perplexed tone, "This is as bad as the swarms of locust in the bible. In the bible. This time God has sent them to eat not our grain, but Emma's gute chocolate cake. Kill them all now! Kill them all."

Tootie took aim with her fist, missed the grasshoppers and accidentally hit the handle of her fork, sending a piece of cake flying through the air. It landed on top of Stella's head and stuck to her prayer cap.

Stella thought it was a grasshopper landing and slapped her head, smashing the cake and icing through her prayer cap. She brought her hand away and stared at the brown goo. "What a mess. What a sticky mess," she said irritably.

Hal bit her bottom lip to keep from grinning as she wondered where the cake came from. Her gaze fell on Tootie. The elderly woman grinned back, pleased with herself. Hal tried to frown, but it was hard to be stern with her aunt. Tootie felt vindicated now that she had gotten back at Stella. Besides, Stella didn't know who flipped the cake on her prayer cap.

The swarm continued for a few minutes before the amount of live insects finally let up. Jane Bontrager leaned back in her chair and held up her red hand. "I am glad we finished the grasshoppers off. My hand is sore."

"Mine, too," Mary Mast agreed as she got up to go see about her baby and the other children. The loud slapping sounds and excited exclamations had startled the little ones on the pallets in the living room. They were crying. She settled the babies down, and patted the toddlers on the back so they would finish their naps. Soon she came back to the kitchen.

Everyone else nodded agreement with Mary as they looked at their sore hands. They leaned back to rest and contemplate what had just happened at the end of this fun day. Embarrassed, Hal worried what the women might think of this insect infestation in the Lapp kitchen.

Margaret Yoder looked across at Mary Mast. Mary smiled and looked at Hal. Hal gave a twitchy smile, and looked dubiously around the table at the others. All of them grinned at each other, then giggled. Finally, they couldn't hold it anymore. They burst into a fit of laughter.

Jane Bontrager wiped at the tears streaming down her face. "I have said it once or twice, but it bears repeating. I can always count on the unexpected and a gute time when Hal Lapp is around."

The way the women laughed, Hal thought they all must agree. She tried to offer an explanation. "I'm sorry this happened. This … this problem was totally unplanned. I can't imagine how so many grasshoppers got in the kitchen."

Hal got up and removed the parsley plant from the window sill to the sink. She inspected the open window for holes in the screen. The screen didn't have any bugs plastered to it, and she couldn't see any holes. Not one grasshopper in the window. She picked up the bushy parsley plant to place it on the sill again and gasped. "Fudge! Here's where they came from. More grasshoppers are hatching out of the soil right now." She raced for the mud room door with the pot and carried it to the back fence.

When Hal returned, she said, "I'm so sorry. I didn't know the pot was full of grasshopper eggs when I brought it in."

"We did not think you did," Margaret said, her lips twitching.

"No harm done," Jane added. "We had most of our cake eaten before the grasshoppers appeared and tracked across the icing."

The women were being good sports about the whole thing. Even Stella Strutt was taking her sticky hair in stride. Just the same, Hal feared the favorite topic around most supper tables that night would be the bug infested Lapp kitchen.

When Rachel's husband, Joe Kitzmiller, drove in, Emma walked with the elderly woman to the buggy. Rachel always needed help to balance when she stepped up. "Denki again for coming to help with the quilt. It is so gute to have it done in one day."

"It was a gute day of fellowship. I enjoyed myself," Rachel said.

"Sure, it was a fun day."

"I imagine I had more of an exciting day here to tell Joe about than Joe did at the salebarn," Rachel said, grinning.

Emma giggled as she helped Rachel into the buggy. Joe gave them a questioning look, wondering what he had missed out on.

Emma asked, "How was your day at the salebarn, Joe?"

"Slow sale day, but I can always find someone to visit with to pass the time," he said, grinning.

"Including my daed, dawdi and brothers I expect."

Joe's sun darken face, woven with wrinkles, scrunched up as he shook his head no. "They were not at the salebarn."

Emma couldn't believe him. "Are you sure?"

"Jah, I am sure."

That was bewildering. Emma excused, "I guess I misunderstood where they were going today. You two, come back to visit any time you can."

"We will do that, and you come visit us," Rachel said.

Joe clapped the lines over his horse. "Get up, Oliver."

As Emma trudged back to the house, she tried to make sense of what she'd just found out. What's going on with the men in her family? That was twice today she found out they had lied about where they disappeared to for a day. She didn't want to upset Hallie and Mammi. This was something she wouldn't mention to them. She just wished she knew why Daed lied. It wasn't like him to do such a thing, and why would Dawdi go along with him, knowing Daed lied. Noah and Daniel hadn't said a thing to her about this. How had they managed to keep what they did a secret? So many questions and no answers.

Chapter 5

Time passed slowly for Emma on the routine days that came and went. Adam hadn't shown up for days. Emma looked out the window every time she heard the clop of hoof beats, hoping it would be Adam.

She missed him more all the time. So much so her thoughts became more troubling with time. Adam might have changed his mind about marrying her. So consumed was she with missing Adam, her worries were fueled by the worse thoughts possible. Thoughts that made Emma quiet and irritable.

One morning, Emma snapped at Daniel for slamming the back door. Hal, Nora and Tootie twisted around to stare at her. Daniel face flushed with embarrassment.

Hal asked," Emma, what's wrong with you?"

"Daniel is no longer a small child that has to be told over and over he should come into the house and leave it without wearing out the screen doors."

"I agree. Now what is really wrong?" Hal persisted.

Emma shrugged. "Just worried about all that we need to get done before the middle of September I reckon." She turned to Daniel. He was shuffling from one bare foot to the other, wishing he could get away. "I am sorry for yelling at you, Daniel. Just try to shut the screen doors easier."

"Are you sure you're edgy because of the wedding plans? Everything is going good. Maybe it's that you're missing

Adam?" Nora wondered. "After all, he hasn't stopped by since we've been here."

"I do miss Adam," Emma admitted.

"Adam told you he was going to be very busy for awhile," Hal said.

"Jah,but knowing that does not stop me from missing him. He should stop by at least long enough to find out how the wedding plans are coming. Sometimes, I feel as if he is staying away on purpose, so he will not have to help us make decisions.

Ach! I'm going to hoe in the garden while it is still cool and cloudy. Weeding helps settle my soul and my temperament. For sure, the Weber sisters garden puts mine to shame. Before they drive by and see mine, I need to do a lot of hoeing," Emma said.

"By all means, give that a try," Hal agreed. As Emma went out the mud room door, she called after her, "But if hoeing doesn't work for you, talk to me about what's bothering you. We're almost finished in the kitchen. We'll be glad to help you hoe if that helps lighten your load."

Tootie hung the dish cloth over the line behind the cook stove and announced, "I'm going to take a nap."

"Right after breakfast! You just got out of bed. Aren't you feeling well?" Nora asked.

Tootie paused in the doorway. With a case of mock weariness, she replied, "Yes, I'm fine, but at my age, when feeling like a nap strikes me, I should take advantage of it."

"Is she all recht?" Hal asked as Tootie disappeared into the clinic.

"I think so. It was either take a nap or let one of us hand her a hoe," Nora said dryly. She walked to the clinic door. "Hal is putting an apple cobbler in the oven. It should be done in an hour. If it wouldn't be too much trouble for you, could you at least check on the cobbler while we're outside? Take it out for us when it's done."

"Yes, I can do that. An hour is just right for a nap," Tootie replied and added a yawn as she sat on the bed.

58

When Tootie returned to the empty kitchen an hour later, she peeked in the oven. The cobbler crust was a golden brown, and the apples bubbled. *Time to take the cobbler out.* She looked at the clock. *In another hour, it will be lunch time. That cobbler should be set somewhere it can cool faster. Nora is always complaining I don't help. This is my chance to be helpful without my bossy sister telling me what to do.*

Tootie took two pot holders from the stack and picked up the cobbler. She backed out the front screen door. After studying the slightly swaying, slatted swing seat, Tootie set the pan on it. With the breeze hitting the pan from the top and the bottom, that should cool off the cobbler.

Tootie glanced over at the garden. Emma, Hal and Nora were hoeing yet, but it looked like they had most of the garden done. Tootie didn't see any reason why she shouldn't lie down again until the women came back in. Twenty minutes later, Tootie heard Nora and Hal talking as they came in the mud room door. She joined them in the kitchen.

Nora nodded at her.

Hal looked into the empty oven as she said, "How was the nap, Aunt Tootie?"

"Fine." Tootie sat down at the table to watch the women work. If they needed her help, they could ask. Why bother to volunteer?

"Mom, … ." Hal looked around the counters and at the table.

"What is it, Hallie?" Nora asked.

"What happened to the apple cobbler? I just looked in the oven. It's not there."

Tootie explained, "You told me to take it out of the oven when it was done. I did what you told me."

Where did you put it, Aunt Tootie?"

"Don't worry … ," Tootie stopped when the front screen door banged.

"Who was it that thought putting our dessert on the porch swing was a gute idea?" Emma demanded, carrying the apple cobbler. She twisted it sideways just enough to let the women see in the pan. Much of the outside crust that had lapped over the apples was missing.

Hal gasped. "What happened to it?"

"Buttercat and Calico made their lunch out of it," Emma said.

"How did the cobbler get outside anyway?" Nora asked.

Tootie bit her lower lip, looking from one to the other. Suddenly, they all stared at her. "Tootie, you were saying before Emma came in that we weren't to worry about the missing apple cobbler. What do you know about this?" Nora pointed at the cobbler.

"I did say that, didn't I?"

After a glance at the clock, Hal supplied, "This close to lunch we have plenty of reasons to worry. We need to come up another dessert."

"Tootie, why did you take the cobber outside?" Nora asked.

"I wanted to cool it down fast. That's all. I can't help it if the cats around here are starved. Hallie, your family should feed the pets better," she accused huffily.

"Gute news, Aendi Tootie. The cats are not hungry now. They ate all they wanted of the crust or could hold and left the rest. I'll feed the apples to the chickens. They have not eaten since early this morning. They must be starve by now, too." Emma stared meaningfully at Tootie before she went out the back door.

Tootie's eyes filled with tears.

Aunt Tootie, we know you didn't expect anything would happen to the apple cobbler. What happened was an accident. If Emma was in a better frame of mind, she'd have realized that." Hal's heart contracted when she thought about the sadness on Emma's face, and she felt sorry for Tootie. The elderly woman looked very dejected after Emma's chewing out.

Hal surprised herself when she came to the rescue. "We have canned applesauce in the basement. That can be dessert."

By the time Emma came back, Hal had two quarts of applesauce, from the basement, on the table and opened. Tootie was spooning the sauce into dessert bowls.

Emma put the baking pan in the dish pan and came to stand

60

by Tootie. "Aendi, I am so sorry I was mean. I do not know what came over me."

Tootie hugged her. "It's all right, dear. We all have a bad day now and then. I forgive you."

The next singing on the in between Sunday, Emma paced the floor waiting for Adam. Buggy wheels crunched the gravel in the driveway. She ran out the front door and stopped at the edge of the porch. Bobby Keim, Adam's brother, parked his buggy in the driveway.

Emma waved. "Wilcom, Bobby. Is Adam coming soon?"

Bobby leveled his serious gaze on her. "Ach, nah! He told me to stop by and pick you up so you would not miss the singing. He does not feel like going tonight."

Emma hurried toward the buggy. "Is he sick?"

"Nah, he is just tired from working so hard. He has another busy week ahead of him," Bobby pushed his straw hat higher on his head so his dark hair showed.

Emma climbed up to the seat. "That is what Adam told me was going to happen. He has had quite a few busy days. I know this must be true, because he has not been over to see me."

Rubbing a finger up and down the lines in his hand, Bobby defended, "Adam feels he has to take the work when he is offered a job. There are times that he does not get jobs for awhile."

That made sense to Emma, except she felt uneasy when Bobby avoided looking at her while he said it. Maybe she imagined he was making up excuses. Making up excuses wasn't like Bobby. She'd have to accept what Adam's brother told her. She didn't have much of a choice.

Bobby parked in the line beside Noah's buggy near the front of Priscilla Tefertiller's barn. The Tefertillers had cleaned out the largest area for the tables and benches.

Bobby and Emma got in line at the snack table to get a cold glass of lemonade before they sat down. Priscilla Tefertiller came up behind Bobby. She reached around him, brushing his arm as she tapped Emma on the shoulder.

Emma was pretty sure Priscilla bumped Bobby deliberately,

so he'd notice her. At least, that was the way it worked. Bobby paid close attention to Priscilla as she talked.

Priscilla smiled down at her bright yellow dress. "Emma, what do you think of my new dress? Do you like the color?"

Canary yellow, a bright color that made Priscilla an attention getter. Oh, and how successfully it worked. Priscilla had Bobby Keim's attention.

"It's pretty," Emma said flatly.

"Adam decided not to come tonight. You are with Bobby, I see," Priscilla said, directing her focus on Bobby.

"Jah," Bobby answered quickly and went on to clarify the reason Emma was with him. "Adam asked me to bring Emma. He needs to get to bed early if he is going to keep up the pace he has set for himself."

"Jah, I guess that is recht," Priscilla agreed. "Adam is working extra hard to finish soon."

Emma had been looking around the room until that remark. "Finish what soon?"

Bobby leveled an intense look at Priscilla. "Jah, Adam has a lot of orders to get done."

Priscilla smiled. "Jah, I know Bobby. It is gute news that business is going so well for Adam." She added. "Gute for me, too. Emma, have you heard? Adam hired me to work as a clerk in his store so he can spend his time in his workshop and on away jobs?"

"Nah, I did not know that." Feeling instantly irritable, it ran through Emma's head, *How could I know when I have not talked to Adam in what seems like forever.* "That is gute news," she answered halfheartedly.

"Gute for me, too." Bobby flashed a smile at Priscilla.

"How is it gute for you?" Emma asked.

"Gets you out of helping your brother, ain't so?" Priscilla teased.

Bobby chuckled as he handed Priscilla a glass of lemonade and filled one for himself. "That and I was thinking I will get to see you every day."

To Emma's chagrin, Priscilla gave Bobby a flirting wink.

Could Adam be thinking the same thing as Bobby? Maybe Priscilla is the real reason he has not been to see me.

Emma said, "I am going to sit down. See you later, Bobby." When she left, Bobby was still talking to Priscilla. Emma scooted onto one of the benches with the single girls and sipped at her lemonade.

Right away, Emma felt out of place. Adam and she had dated for a long time. They always shared one of the benches for couples. It didn't help that she caught girls staring at her as if she'd picked the wrong bench.

The flurry of whispers were hard to ignore. Emma expected to hear them murmuring to each other that she'd broken up with Adam. She stared straight at the whispers, daring them to wondered if she was going to end up a maidel.

Noah and Jenny Yoder sat at one of the couples tables. Her brother must have finally got up enough courage to ask Jenny to go to the singing with him. Noah noticed where Emma was seated and frowned. Emma gave him a weak smile and looked away.

During the break, everyone lined up at the snack table for lemonade and chocolate chip cookies. Emma noticed Daniel asked Jimmie Miller's sister, Ella, if she'd like to eat with him. Her little brother was growing up and ready to date.

Levi Yoder and Katie Yost came over to Emma's table while she nibbled on her cookie. After some small talk, Katie said she was sorry Adam didn't make it to the singing.

"Adam is busy working long hours," Emma said, repeating the only answer she had. Actually, she wondered, *Is Katie afraid she made the bridesmaid dress for nothing?*

Emma excused herself. She threw her paper plate and Dixie cup into the trash can and headed out the door. She needed fresh air in the worst way and to be alone. For a few minutes, she'd get away from all the curious looks and questions that were sure to keep coming. She'd be so glad when this night ended.

The evening was pleasant and quiet except for the incessant cricket chirps. The moon, full and white, cast a silvery glow on the surroundings. Millions of stars glittered the sky. Emma took a deep breath and wished Adam could enjoy the night with her.

Noah slipped up behind her. "Everything all recht, Emma?" Emma recognized his voice. She didn't turn around. "Jah."

"You seem troubled to me," Noah worried.

Emma turned to him and folded her arms at the waist. "Ach, nah! I am just missing Adam is all."

"He must be busy, or he would be here," Noah said.

"That is what Bobby told me. Adam sent him to pick me up."

"Why are you out here alone?"

"I just needed a breath of fresh air. You go back in and enjoy the evening with Jenny. I am glad you brought her tonight. I will be in before the next round of singing starts," Emma assured him.

As soon as Noah went inside, Emma walked out of the glow from the building doorway and leaned against the wall. Hopefully, no one else would see her.

Familiar voices came from around the corner of the barn. She wasn't alone. Emma edged toward the direction of the voices. She peeked around the barn and recognized the dark figures of Bobby and Priscilla, standing close together.

Most couples usually went off by themselves during break. Adam and she usually did the same thing. She had a hard time thinking of pretty, man magnet Priscilla and quiet, hard working Bobby Keim as a couple. She hoped that Priscilla didn't hurt Bobby by leading him on. He was just coming out of his shell after the loss of Anna Hosteller. Emma wanted him to be happy again.

A sharp pang of missing Adam welled up in her as she started to go back inside. That's when she heard Bobby mention her name. She paused to listen.

"I thought for a minute you were going to say more than you should to Emma," Bobby cautioned.

"It is a gute thing you stopped me. From now on, I will try real hard not to say anything to her that will give this away.

Adam should tell her himself. No reason that I can see to keep this a secret for so long. It is not fair to Emma. She needs to know, so she will stop worrying," Priscilla said.

"I do not agree with Adam, but it is his decision to make," Bobby replied. "For now, I am staying out of his business. Just be careful what you say around Emma if you do not want Adam upset with you."

A heated, flushed feeling, like when she stood over the black kettle of boiling water on chicken butchering day, roiled in the pit of Emma's stomach. Was Adam so scared of getting married he was trying to back out in the only way he knew how? By distancing himself from her, did he hope she'd get tired of waiting for him and call the wedding off? Adam had discussed his problem with his brother and Priscilla of all people. He could come talk to her. She'd understand. They didn't have to get married until Adam was ready.

Emma edged along the front of the barn and backed into a warm body. Startled, her hand went to her throat. She let out a soft gasp.

Noah said, "Take it easy. It is just me."

She whirled around and hissed, "I see that now. I thought you went back inside. I did not know anyone was around."

Noah sounded baffled. "Reckon not. Hard to see me behind you when you are backing up."

"Jenny will be wondering why you keep leaving her. We better go inside now," Emma insisted, flustered.

"Are you sure you are all recht?"

"Jah, I am sure. Stop asking me," Emma said irritably.

"You are acting strange."

"I am not," Emma hissed, pushing Noah toward the door. "I told you I just came out for a breath of fresh air. I am going back inside recht now."

"All recht, lets go," Noah said.

Emma hesitated at the door to make sure Bobby and Priscilla weren't in sight. She didn't want them to know she'd eavesdropped on them.

She made it back to the singles bench before Bobby and

Priscilla appeared in the doorway. They stayed together and settled in at one of the couples tables. For the latter part of the evening, she managed to sing the songs, but her heart wasn't in it.

Thoughts of what she heard by the barn and what problem must be bothering Adam swirled through her head. On the way home, Emma asked, "Bobby, are you and Priscilla going out now?"

"Jah, I am going to court Priscilla."

After that, Emma remained quiet until they reached her house. She thanked him for being so thoughtful to pick her up for the singing and hurried inside before the crunch of Bobby's buggy wheels faded away.

Chapter 6

On Monday afternoon, Emma couldn't stand not knowing what was going on. She had to talk to Adam. She told Hal, "I am going over to see how Adam is coming with remodeling our apartment over the shop. I hope he has it about done so he can stop working so hard."

"All recht. Tell Adam hi for us," Hal said.

When Emma parked by the shop, the only other buggy there was Priscilla's. Emma recognized it as hers. Priscilla had been driving one of the new fiberglass, see through, enclosed buggies lately.

When the door opened, Priscilla stopped dusting a bookcase. "Hello, Emma."

"I want to talk to Adam." Emma rushed across the room to the work room door.

"No need to go in there," Priscilla said emphatically.

Emma ignored Priscilla as she opened the door. She wanted to see the furniture Adam had been working on for the English house. The room was half full of glistening pine furniture. "Adam is not here."

"That is what I was going to tell you," Priscilla replied.

"It looks like Adam has the order finished for an English customer." Emma rubbed the slick surface of the square dining room table. Leaning against the wall were three leaves used to make the table larger. Eight stacked chairs matched the table.

Two rockers were next in line. A simple bed head and foot leaned against the wall behind the table.

Puzzled, Emma turned to find Priscilla eying her intently. "These pieces are almost too plain for an English customer."

Priscilla's eyes moved back and forth as she shrugged. "Uh, ... I reckon that is the new English style these days. Keep the furniture simple like the Amish do."

Emma came to stand in front of Priscilla. "Ach, is so?"

Priscilla moved away from the door opening. Emma walked past her and started up the stairs.

"No need to go up there. Adam is not there, either."

"I just want to look," Emma retorted over her shoulder. She opened the door at the top of the stairs and walked into the space over the shop. The area was empty except for two rockers Adam had sanded and a partially used can of varnish.

Emma turned in a circle, trying to take in the fact the space hadn't been divided into rooms. Maybe this was another sign he changed his mind about marrying her. He didn't see any reason to work on a home if he wasn't getting married. She slowly walked back down the stairs.

Waiting at the bottom, Priscilla stared up at her. "Emma, you looked peaked. Are you feeling all recht?"

Emma didn't answer.

"Was ist letz?" Priscilla asked, alarmed.

With a grip on the railing, Emma stated dully, "Adam was going to build an apartment above the shop for us to live in. He has not started it."

"Adam has been very busy, lately" Priscilla repeated weakly.

"I have heard that excuse many times now, but busy doing what? Certainly not getting a home ready for us. Certainly not coming over to see me to find out about the wedding plans. The wedding date is too soon. I do not see how he could possibly get the apartment done in time now," Emma said dully. Her mind searched for an explanation.

"Ach, Emma! You need to talk to Adam. Do not get upset. He can explain," Priscilla said, rubbing the banister in one spot nervously with the dust rag.

"Stop rutschiching around with that rag. You are hiding something from me. You say Adam can explain, but I want to know when does he wish to face me and do it? Priscilla, why are you so nervous?"

"I think you do not like me. That makes me nervous," Priscilla said bluntly.

"Ach, Priscilla, you are so full of yourself I do not think about you at all. Lately when you do come to mind, I remember how loose you were with Eli Yutzy, and I worry for Bobby." Priscilla's eyes fired up. Emma knew she hit a nerve. "Bobby cared so much for Anna Hosteller. He is just getting over that loss and does not need to be hurt again. What worries me, when I think of you, is your intentions now that you are going out with him. Not only that, now it wonders me that you are employed here. Have you something planned for Adam as well as Bobby? Are you just playing both of them, waiting to see which man takes the bait?" Emma descended the few steps left and rushed passed Priscilla to the door.

Once she was in the buggy, she gave Ben his head. Pride saved her from tears in front of Priscilla, but alone in the buggy, her eyes filled and flooded over. Pent up tears of fear that she might be losing Adam, and tears of helpless anger that she might be losing him to flirty Priscilla streamed down her face.

Before she pulled into the Lapp driveway, Emma bit her lower lip and breathed deeply in order to stop crying. She didn't want Hal and the others to see how upset she was. If she could make it passed them, she'd go to her room until she calmed down.

The next Sunday worship meeting was at Joe Kitzmiller's farm. Emma watched for Adam, but he didn't come to the service. The Keim farm was a half mile away. Bobby and his mother, Lovina, came. It was not like Adam to miss a Sunday worship service, but maybe Priscilla had talked to him about her visit. Priscilla wasn't at the service either, but that wasn't unusual. She wasn't a member of the church so she missed occasionally.

As soon as the service was over, Emma searched the room for Lovina Keim, Adam's mother. She was among a group of women entering the kitchen to serve up the fellowship lunch. Emma hurried to catch her, but Bishop Bontrager made it to Lovina first. Emma stopped. She was close enough to hear as Elton Bontrager pulled the stick thin woman aside. "I noticed Adam was not here today. Is he sick?"

Lovina crossed her arms over her chest. She looked toward the kitchen like she'd rather be working. "Nah, Adam is not sick. He is just very busy."

The bishop probed, "He is not working on the Lord's day?"

"Ach, nah. He would not do that. To tell you the truth, Bishop, he is avoiding Emma. She has so many questions, and he does not know how to answer her truthfully."

Emma tensed. She had to listen intently to catch every word above all the chatter surrounding her. So Adam was avoiding her. She hadn't imagined it.

"I met John Lapp on the road yesterday. He told me Emma is really upset. She does not know why Adam is not spending time with her, and she is very worried. Adam should talk to her before long," Elton Bontrager said. "This is not fair to Emma."

"I did not realize Emma was so worried. I will tell Adam what you have said. He must talk to her," Lovina said.

"Jah, and tell Adam for me, it may be difficult to wait on the Lord at a Sunday service, but it is worse to wish he had."

"I will tell him," Lovina agreed.

Emma stayed where she was until Lovina mingled among the kitchen workers. She didn't want Adam's mother to catch her eavesdropping. When was all the secrecy going to end?

There were plenty of helpers in the kitchen. They didn't need her, and Emma needed time alone. She walked outside and along the side of the house. She could sit in the grass and think. It was shady, and the breeze was cool. She sat down with her legs curled to the side and picked at clover leaves, looking for a four leaf clover.

Katie Yost and Jennie Yoder burst around the house. Katie said, "There you are. We have been looking for you, Emma."

"Why?"

"We wanted to talk to you. Why are you out here by yourself?" Jennie asked.

Emma shrugged. "I just felt like being alone is all."

"We hadn't had a chance to see you away from everyone," Katie said. "I wanted to tell you I have my dress and apron made."

Jennie added, "Me, too."

Emma nodded. "Jah, I sewed mine so all three are done. That is gute."

Jennie studied her. "You do not look happy. Are you troubled about something?"

Emma sighed as she raised her head toward the sky. "Jah, I am."

"Is there something wrong between you and Adam?" Katie asked.

"Adam has been working a lot I hear. I have not seen him for days," Emma said.

"That is what we hear, too," Katie said.

"Jah. At least, you are not just sitting home. You still come to the singings. That is gute," Jennie encouraged.

"Jah, it is something to do to keep busy until Adam has time to go with you," Katie said.

"No need to go to the singings anymore," Emma said dully. "I have been spending as many evenings as I can with my grandparents and aunt. I would not go to the singings after I marry so I might as well stop now."

"Jah, maybe. So nothing is really wrong between you and Adam," Katie persisted.

"I really do not know. I worry. I miss Adam, but I cannot find him to talk to him. He is never home, and today he did not show up for the service. I feel like he is avoiding me. Do either of you know something about Adam that I should be told?"

"Nah, nothing that we *should* tell you," Katie said, looking at Jennie.

"You are worrying for nothing," Jennie said adamantly.

"What if Adam has decided not to marry me? I should be

told that instead of excuses about how busy he is while he hides from me," Emma fretted.

"If that is what you think Adam is doing, you are wrong," Jennie said sternly.

"You are certain of that."

"Jah, Adam is very much in love with you. He is going to marry you," Jennie assured her.

"Jah, give him a chance to get caught up with his work. He will be done soon," Katie said.

Emma eyed her intently. "What work is he going to finish soon, Katie?"

Katie shrugged. "Uh … whatever it is that is keeping him so busy. I cannot say."

Emma probed, "How is it you are so sure Adam will be done soon, Katie? How do you know that, and I do not?"

"Well …. well," Katie looked at Jennie. Jennie was biting her lower lip to keep silent. "It is just something I heard from Levi."

"What did you hear?"

Katie looked so cornered that Jennie interrupted. "Adam will be less busy soon. Levi told me that, too."

"I hear many conversations happened between people that know what Adam is doing. I feel like I am in the dark about something. Have either of you seen Adam out with another woman?"

"Stop that recht now!" Jennie snapped. "If you heard anything, it could not have been that."

"Adam would not do that to you," Katie declared.

"All recht, so do you think I should be patient just a little longer?" Emma asked.

"Jah! That really is the best thing to do. You will be a married woman come September 15th. You will see." Jennie gave her a hug. "Come on, we should join the others."

That evening, Emma got ready for the singing. She'd go by herself if Adam didn't come. At the sound of horse hooves, Emma peeked out. Bobby Keim drove in. This time he drove the two seated carriage. On the front seat, he had his date,

72

Priscilla Tefertiller.

Emma hated to see Bobby with Priscilla, but he hadn't asked her for advice. She wasn't a bit surprised that Priscilla's flirting ways finally worked with Bobby. She just hoped it wasn't working on Adam as well.

Priscilla was unhappy to see her walk to the buggy. Emma knew it would be uncomfortable to make small talk with Bobby and try to ignore his date's angry glares.

Not to mention, she'd feel uncomfortable riding with the newly dating couple. She turned down Bobby's offer for a ride to the singing. She excused she'd rather stay home and visit with her grandparents and aunt.

Noah listened from the porch. When Bobby drove away, he went to meet Emma. "You can ride with Daniel and me to the singing. I can see going with Bobby and Priscilla on their date would be awkward."

"Denki, Noah, but you are taking Jenny Yoder, ain't so?"

"Nah, she is going with her brother, Mark, tonight."

"Not wanting to go with Bobby and Priscilla is only one reason I told Bobby I was staying home. I just cannot stand to hear the girls buzz like cicadas, full of questions and rumors about Adam and me. I do not have answers for them. Better that I stay home until I find out what is wrong with Adam."

Noah regarded her calmly for a moment. His voice was crisp. "Nothing is wrong with Adam. When he says he is busy you should believe him."

"Do you know something that I do not?" Emma asked sharply.

Jah, you worry too much and needlessly," Noah said, his composure guarded as he walked away from her. "I have to go hitch up Mike so Daniel and me can leave."

After devotions, Nora and Tootie followed Hal to the kitchen to help serve a cake. Nora wondered out loud, "Something bothering Emma? She hasn't been humming like she used to while she works."

Tootie added, "It's not like her to miss a singing."

Hal concentrated on slicing the applesauce cake. "I'm not

sure what's ailing Emma."

Tootie said, "I think it is wedding jitters."

"Perhaps, that is it," Hal agreed, but she made a mental note to talk to Emma when they were alone to find out for sure. Maybe something had happened she didn't know about.

Hal got her chance while they hung clothes on the line the next morning. Emma worked, but she had a far away look on her face. Definitely, her mind was somewhere else.

Hal shook out a shirt and penned it to the line. "Emma, you want to talk about what's wrong?"

Emma pushed the basket holder a few feet ahead. Then she hung up a shirt. "What makes you think anything is wrong?"

Hal shook out a shirt and reached in the bag for two pens. "Apparently, I'm not the only one that noticed you seem upset. Mom and Aunt Tootie mentioned to me they're worried about you."

"Ach! If all of you have noticed, I reckon I should tell you. I need to talk about this to someone before I bust." She dropped the shirt back in the basket and fisted her hands on her hips. "I suppose you noticed Adam hasn't been to see me for a long time."

"Jah. I hear he's busy."

"That is what I have been told over and over already until now it sounds like excuses."

"But …. ." Hal began.

Emma interrupted, "I worry Adam would make time for me like he always did if not for a problem. I think Adam might not want to marry me anymore."

Hal looked shocked. "You think he's getting cold feet?"

"I do not know if his feet are cold, and recht now I do not care," Emma said irritably.

Hal tried not to grin. "Nah, I mean you think he has changed his mind."

"That is what I just sort of said."

"Have you mentioned this to Adam? You went to see him, recht? I can't believe he'd change his mind after all the years he has waited for you to marry him."

74

"I did go to the store. Adam was not there. His *sales clerk*, Priscilla Tefertiller, was. Can you imagine he picked her of all women to hire?

I went upstairs to see how our apartment looks. He has not even started it. Where are we supposed to live? I checked in the work room. He has the English order of furniture done that was keeping him so busy."

"How about Eve Weber's kitchen?"

"I do not know if he has finished that or not?"

You know what I think. You need to have faith in the man you're going to marry," Hal said bluntly. "If he says he's busy working, he is busy."

"I wish I had your kind of faith in Adam, but what if Adam has changed his mind? I do not want him to wait until the last minute and embarrass me and my family by not showing up at the wedding. That would be so humiliating."

"Ach! Adam definitely wouldn't do that. He isn't that kind of man," declared Hal emphatically.

Emma persisted, "I hope not, but what if he is?"

"You shouldn't say such things about Adam," Hal insisted.

Emma looked sullen. "I cannot help it."

"All recht! Obviously, you aren't going to take my word for it that Adam is an honorable man. I don't know what his work schedule is so I can't help you there. I think you should talk to Bishop Bontrager. See if he can make some sense out of your worries," Hal suggested.

Emma perked up at the suggestion. "Jah, I can do that. I'll go by his house and see if he has time to talk to me."

That night after everyone had gotten in bed, Hal tossed and turned.

John lifted his head and rested on his hand so he could gaze down at her. "What ails you?"

Hal whispered, "I'm worried about Emma."

"Why?"

"Emma hasn't been herself lately. Finally this morning, I got her to talk to me."

"And?"

"Emma's worried about why Adam is staying away. It's not like him to ignore her like this and for this long. She thinks Adam wants to back out on their wedding. I tried to tell her Adam wouldn't do that to her. If he said he's working, he is. She should trust him."

"That was the recht things to say. Adam is completely trustworthy. He loves Emma, and she should know that by now without us telling her," John said, sounding irritated.

"Ach, John, you are recht, but Emma didn't believe me. You talk to her. Tell her you trust Adam."

"Ach, nah! I do not think I want to do that."

"Why not? Your words means a lot to your daughter," Hal said.

"Emma is full grown now although she does not act like it lately. She needs to work out her feelings by herself. You just said she did not listen to you."

"Jah, and I ran out of ideas so I suggested Emma talk to the bishop. Maybe he can help her understand she has to be patient with Adam. I hate to see her treat that hard working man this way behind his back," Hal shared.

"Sounds like the recht thing to do. Now go to sleep. Worrying does not help, ain't so? You need your rest." John kissed her gently on the cheek. By the moonlight shining through the window, Hal could see he had a one sided quirk to his mouth. "Good night, Hal."

She turned onto her side and closed her eyes. Her last thought was, *How could John be so calm about Emma and Adam's problem when the wedding is so close? That was a strange expression he just gave me. Does he know something I don't?*

The next morning, Emma announced she was going for a ride. Only Hal knew where she was headed. Jane Bontrager greeted her at the front door with a hug. Elton was drinking coffee at the kitchen table. "Gute to see you, Emma. Come sit down."

"Want a cup of coffee?" Jane asked in her gentle voice as she sat down in front of her cup.

"Nah, I am not thirsty. Do you have a moment to talk with me, Bishop?"

"Jah, and maybe two if you need them. I've been expecting you. Your father told me you have been fretting about something to do with Adam." The bishop, his complexion very red with concern, gave her a once over look. "You are not eating enough to keep a bird alive from the look of you. Worry will make you lose your appetite." Elton said knowingly, "I can see you are troubled by something. Was ist letz?"

"I do not know where else to turn, Bishop. Hallie said maybe you could give me some advice. Worrisome thoughts about Adam nag at me all the time. As soon as we started discussing wedding plans, Adam has not been to see me except for taking me to two singings. I have this awful fear that he might not want to marry me anymore. I wonder if he's avoiding me, because he is having a hard time finding a way to tell me."

"Ach, Emma! Surely not. That does not sound like something Adam would do," Jane cried.

Elton frowned as he clasped his short, plump fingers together. "Emma, when you agreed to marry Adam, you trusted him to do what is recht by you, ain't so?"

"Jah."

"I believe Adam Keim to be a man of his word. Has he ever as long as you have known him given you any cause to doubt that he was a gute and honorable man?"

"Nah."

"Has anyone given you a reason why Adam has not come to see you lately?" Jane asked, her brown eyes filled with friendly warmth.

"Jah, everyone I talk to says Adam is working. The last time I saw Adam he told me he had a lot of work to do."

Bishop Bontrager persisted, "But now, you have too much time alone on your hands. You miss Adam so you have become a doubting Thomas, because Adam is not spending time with you."

"A doubting Thomas?"

"You need to read your bible about the disciple Thomas when you get home. He was the first doubting Thomas. He should have had more faith in Jesus just like you need to have faith in Adam if you truly want to marry him."

Emma wiped a tear off her cheek. "If I could just talk to Adam, I would feel so much better."

"That is almost the words Thomas said to the other disciples when he didn't believe them. Thomas demanded proof that Jesus had risen from the dead and was walking among them. So I suspect if Adam stopped what he is doing and came to talk to you it would not help you. No matter what Adam told you now, if you do not believe in the man, you say you love, you will still find a reason to worry when he is not where you can see him."

Emma's eyes flooded with tears. "What should I do, Bishop?"

There was a note of gruff kindness in his voice. "Pray to God for the strength to trust Adam. He deserves your blinding faith and trust."

"I will pray, but can you tell me anything about what Adam is doing that keeps him away from me? You are out in the community. You hear and see things."

"There is nothing I can tell you. Trust in the Lord and in your soon to be husband," Elton said earnestly.

Jane patted Emma's hand. "Elton is recht. Trust Adam and all will work out. You have much to do, preparing for the wedding and little time left. It is best to concentrate on that, and stop worrying about what is over the horizon. That is God's work."

Elton and Jane's advice didn't make Emma feel better. They didn't solve her worries, but she vowed to try to do as the bishop said. She would pray.

Emma closed the screen door and paused on the Bontrager front porch, wondering when she'd ever feel happy again. In the kitchen, she heard her name mentioned. Jane and Elton were talking about her.

Jane said, "Poor Emma. Adam really should not keep her in

the dark like this."

"Ordinarily, I would say you are recht, but Emma should have more faith in the man she loves. It surprises me she does not. If her faith is not strong enough to believe in Adam now, maybe they should not get married after all."

Emma walked to the buggy, stunned by the bishop's words. Elton and Jane's conversation certainly didn't make her feel any better. They knew something about Adam. She asked, and they deliberately didn't tell her.

She was sure Adam was avoiding her, but why? What was it everyone but her knew about Adam and weren't willing to share with her? Was the bishop serious when he said she and Adam should not get married if she didn't trust Adam? The bishop had to be wrong. Her faith in Adam had always been strong. It would be again if she could just get Adam to explain to her what he'd been doing all this time away from her.

Chapter 7

The last day of June, early in the morning, the sky clouded over and let go with a gentle shower. The Amish community was thankful for the rain. They needed moisture to make their garden and field crops flourish.

Just as the rain ceased, a buggy stopped in the Lapp driveway. An Amish farmer ran to the clinic, his long gray beard flopping on his chest. He knocked hard on the door.

Hal rushed from the living room to let him in. "Wilcom, Hiram Mast. Come in."

The farmer's fuzzy gray eyebrows furrowed together. "Nah, I cannot stay. I just wondered if you wanted to take a look at Rudy Briskey."

"What's wrong with him?"

"I just went by his cornfield while it was still raining. He was down between the rows, flat out like he was unconscious."

"You didn't stop to check on him?"

"Nah, I would not know what to do for him so I came to get you," Hiram answered as he hurried down the porch steps.

"Denki for stopping. I'll go see about him." Hal rushed to the cupboard for her nursing bag.

Emma appeared in the doorway.

"Emma, you want to go with me? Hiram Mast says Rudy Briskey is laying in his cornfield."

"Jah, I heard, I will hook Ben up to the buggy."

Soon Hal drove east on the road and turned at the intersection. The Briskey farm was a quarter mile down that road. Hal drove the buggy into the field driveway closest to the house and parked at the edge of the corn rows. She looked across the rows of small green shoots. "Do you see anything, Emma?"

Emma shaded her eyes with her hand from the sun's glare. "Nah, I do not."

"What are you two trying to see?" The booming male voice of Rudy Briskey so close beside the buggy made Hal and Emma jump.

Ben blew and tossed his head, startled by Rudy's loudness.

Hal pulled back on the lines. "My goodness! Easy, Ben." She stuck her head out the driver's window. "Rudy, you startled us. Are you all recht?"

"Jah, why would I not be?" Rudy asked impatiently, rubbing his long, brown beard.

"Hiram Mast stopped by. He told me to check on you. He said you passed out in the corn rows."

Rudy burst out laughing and slapped his leg. "That is a gute story. Maybe Hiram should have stopped to check on me himself. That would have save you the bother of driving all the way over here.

I am all recht. A gute shower came up while I hoed weeds. I was so glad to see it, alls I did was flop down on the ground to enjoy nature's wonder. While I was flat, I praised God for the moisture to my crops. Is anything wrong with that?"

"Nah, that is a gute thing. We are glad you are all recht. Now we best get back to our company. See you at worship service next," Emma said.

Hal slapped the reins against Ben's back and pulled toward her to get him to back out of the driveway. "We better leave before he thinks he owes me two more sheep for a home visit. John wouldn't like it if I brought home anymore of Rudy's scrubs."

That set them both to laughing, but all too soon, Emma's laughter faded. Her mind went back to what had been bothering her for days as she stared out the windshield.

Hal glanced at Emma, wishing the girl wasn't so troubled. After all, this should be a happy time in her life. "How did your visit with Bishop Bontrager go yesterday?"

"The bishop was not much help, but he tried. He stuck up for Adam more than he sympathized with me. Elton called me a doubting Thomas for not trusting Adam. He said I should pray for the strength to believe in Adam if I really intended to marry him. Jane agreed with Elton."

"Sounds like gute advice to me. We all believe Adam is a gute, hard working man, and I shouldn't have to remind you that you believe that, too."

"Ach jah, and I almost believed all that Bishop Bontrager said. That was before I overheard him and Jane, in the kitchen, talking as I was ready to leave their porch. They know something they would not tell me. Jane told Elton I should know. Elton said it was Adam's place to tell me. He could not do it."

"What were they talking about I wonder?" Hal mused.

"Whatever it was, Bobby Keim and Priscilla Tefertiller had almost the same conversation at the singing at the Tefertiller farm three weeks ago. I overheard them talking. They agreed I should know something about Adam, but Adam should tell me."

"Are you sure you aren't making too much out of what you heard?"

"Nah, at the last worship service, Bishop was talking to Lovina Keim. He was concerned, because Adam was not there. Elton wanted to know if Adam was working on the Lord's day. Lovina said he wasn't. Adam was just avoiding me. Hallie, I cannot take not knowing what is going on much longer."

Hal grimaced. "Sounds like you have been doing entirely too much eavesdropping on everyone, Schnuppich."

Emma gave her a stern look. "All recht, but I was not snooping on purpose. What I heard was by accident."

Hal put her arm around Emma's shoulders and hugged her. "I understand completely. Still I don't think Adam is the kind of man to hurt you intentionally."

"Exactly why he has not gotten up the nerve to face me yet. Adam does not want to marry me, and he is avoiding me. I feel as if my future is at stake here. If that is it, Adam should be man enough to tell me the wedding is off," Emma groaned, twisting her hands in her lap. "Otherwise, Adam should want me to know we have a roof over our heads somewhere. Maybe it is with his mother and Bobby for awhile. That is all recht. I just want to know.

He should be interested to know how I worked it out so I have September off when school starts. It is as if he has not given any thought to how important teaching is to me. If he was interested, he would be discussing these details with me."

"Ach, dear Emma! You have spent your whole life being a worrier, and I fear you will never stop. Did you know that?"

Emma's eyes widened as she shook her head no.

"You've carried the load for everyone. That has to stop. At a very young age, you took care of your mother and worried about how she affected all of you. After she died, you were saddled with raising your brothers and taking care of your father. You worried about all of them all the time.

Your father married me, a hopeless excuse for a homemaker, and you constantly worry about me. There wasn't time to be a girl with a life of your own until you met Adam. Now you're worried about him. Give the man a break. He's going to marry you. Soon he'll be the head of your house and taking care of you. You won't have to worry so much then. Not that any of us will ever be able to stop you.

As for now, don't make yourself sick over what you don't know. Take care of what you do know. You need to think about yourself. You're getting married. I'm sure of it. This should be a wonderful moment in your life. Try to look forward to it. Concentrate on it, and let Adam take care of where you're going to live."

Emma folded her arms at her waist and looked at the road. Her tone was cryptic. "I will try, but it will not be easy. Someone in the Lapp family has always had to have a level head and worry that everything goes recht for all of us. If only there was a way to blank out unwelcome thoughts. So far I have not found it."

Hal decided to give up. She realized she hadn't said anything that made a difference in Emma's mind. She wanted to be in control of everything happening around her. No one was going to convince her not to be.

During July, the days were usually hot and dry in southern Iowa. By the fourth of July, the day started out sultry, the precursor to a storm.

When it finally did get around to storming, John predicted it would be a humdinger, but he prayed for rain anyway. They hadn't gotten measurable rain the last two weeks of June. His crops were in need of a good soaking.

That morning, Hal and Nora sat in the swing on the porch, snapping green beans. It was cooler there than in the house. Under the maple tree, Tootie perched in a chair, like a queen on her throne, supposedly watching Redbird and Beth playing on a quilt. Emma was in the kitchen washing jars, and getting the pressure canner water heated.

Tootie paid more attention to the chickens in front of the barn, then she did the girls. Abraham scratched at a horse pile and clucked excitedly. From all directions, hens ran to see what he had to eat, and so did Tom Turkey. They pecked, scratched and fought over the fleeing bugs.

"Hallie, that turkey is getting really close to us," complained Tootie.

Nora said, "Tootie, just ignore him. He isn't one bit interested in you as long as the rooster keeps finding him bugs to eat."

John and Jim came out of the barn.

Hal called, "How's the cow?"

"Won't be long now before we have a new calf." John looked at the cloudless sky. "Hal, I am going to check the hay field." He turned back to his father-in-law. "Want to walk along, Jim?"

The elderly man fell into step beside John. "You bet. As much good food as I'm eating lately, I need all the exercise I can get."

John whistled for the dog. Biscuit crawled out from under a buggy in the lean-to and stretched. He caught up to the men, passed them than stopped to lift his leg and wet down a wooden fence post. After that, he loped off ahead of the men, reached the hay field and scared up a rabbit. Biscuit gave chase until the rabbit dove down a hole. He ambled back to the men and heeled behind them.

Part way down the lane, John kicked at a seeded out button weed that was only a few inches high. "That is not gute."

"Weeds know when to mature early in dry weather, don't they?" Jim commented.

John gazed across his cornfield. "Jah. Emma's wedding is right when I should start harvesting, but I might not have to worry about storing a large crop of corn if it stays this dry. Reckon everything happens for the best."

"Now don't start worrying about how you're going to get the corn picked. We aren't in any hurry to leave. I can help you get the corn in after the wedding and be glad to do it," Jim volunteered.

"That is kind of you. Alls this will work out. Ach, I am not much of a farmer anyway," John said humbly as Amish farmers do. He stepped out into his large hay field to survey it. "What do you think?"

"The plants aren't as tall as they ought to be, but second cuttings are never as productive as the first. Third is even worse."

"Jah, but the alfalfa leaves are starting to wilt from the heat." John pointed at his feet. "Big cracks in the ground is not gute."

A rumble came from the west, low and lengthy.

"Where did that noise come from?" John asked.

"Right out of the blue for sure." Jim shaded his eyes and looked toward the distant gravel road. "Maybe a wagon's passing by."

John took notice of the sky. "Nah, a storm is coming. Look

85

at that thunderhead building."

Jim chuckled. "By golly, it's as black as the ace of spades. Looks like you're going to get that rain you been praying for. Reckon we best head for the house while we're still dry."

Under the maple tree, Tootie pulled her dress front out away from her chest. She complained, "I'm so clammy with sweat my dress is sticking to me. Those poor chickens and that turkey are so hot. Their mouths are wide open, panting."

"We all feel just like you and the chickens do, Tootie. Try not to think about it," Nora said, throwing the end of a green bean and stem in a bucket between Hal and her.

"Aunt Tootie, when Mom and I get done, we can all stop to have a glass of ice tea," Hal said, breaking a green bean into her pan.

Does the Amish celebrate the fourth?" Nora asked Hal, hoping a subject change would help them forget about how hot the day was.

"Independence Day is thought of as an English holiday. Given that the Amish don't consider themselves patriotic, it's not a holiday for them," Hal explained. "They have a holiday of their own called Ascension day the last of May. We went to the picnic grove that day. The Yoder family came over, and everyone fished. It was a day of rest and fun."

"What's the holiday for?" Nora asked.

"It is to celebrate the ascension day of Christ and happens forty two days after Easter."

The sticky breeze picked up and blew the welcome scent of rain dampened earth at them. Hal set her pan on the floor and walked over to the end of the porch. She put her hand on the wall and leaned over to looked behind the house. Thick, black, low hanging clouds were rolling in from the northwest.

"Listen to the thunder," Hal said. "A storm is coming. John will be pleased to see the rain."

The low rumbles of thunder came close together in the distance.

"Let's moved the pots of beans to the basement to finish

snapping them. It will be cooler down there maybe," Hal suggested. She yelled, "Emma, it's going to rain. Can you come out and help Aunt Tootie with the girls. They need to go to the basement to play. Mom and I will close the house windows."

"Jah," Emma called out the kitchen window before she shut it.

No longer than it took the men to walk back to the house, the black storm spread over much of the sky. Spears of lightning diced though the dense cloud cover. The wind turned from gusts to strong, swift moans, swaying harshly through the high branches of the maple tree.

Suddenly, the violent wind seemed to whip from all directions at once. Leaning into the wind, John and Jim held their straw hats on their heads. Their trousers whipped around their legs.

"This storm bears watching," John said gravely.

"That it does," Jim agreed. "The lightning is sharp. Regular sky busters for sure."

John pointed to a tail sticking out near the base at the front of the roiling, dark cloud. "Watch that white tail swing down."

"That's a tornado brewing if I ever saw one," Jim agreed. "Quite a combination coming at us. The green on the front of that cloud I'd say means wind and hail."

"We better get the women and kids to the basement." John ran for the front door. He burst into the empty kitchen. "Hal, where are you?"

"In the basement. What's wrong?" Hal called up the stairs.

John shouted at the open basement door. "A tornado is headed at us. Where are the boys?"

"In the barn. They went to check on the cow again," Emma said.

"All of you stay put. I am going to get the boys and be recht down," John said.

Outside, he braced himself to stand upright in the wind and tried to make his voice heard over the roar as he called his boys' names.

Daniel looked out the barn door and said something over his

shoulder to Noah.

"Get to the house quick. Storm coming." John pointed behind him.

Noah appeared behind Daniel. They looked where John pointed. The black cloud's white swirling tail spiraled closer to the ground. It took both boys, fighting against the wind, to close the barn doors.

They ran to the house and tramped down the basement steps. John and the boys joined Jim at the window that faced the west. From there, they watched the storm approach.

Bright flashes of lightning repeatedly cracked, and thunder boomed a reply. Suddenly, rain poured down in sheets. Redbird and Beth whimpered and hugged when the wind and rain pelted the house. Hal picked up Beth, and Nora lifted Redbird into her arms.

The gale force winds sweep over everything in the storm's path, raising debris and dust into the air. The tornado seemed like a large black whip snapped down from the clouds as it landed a mile from the Lapp farm. The vortex of whirling debris and dirt veered off to the southeast.

John said in amazement, "That is a whole wagon flying in the air, ain't so?"

"It is, and look! There goes a tree or the biggest part of one," Jim said excitedly.

"Holy buckets! I hope that big tree at the end of the house doesn't blow over on us," Tootie exclaimed.

"It would not do that, ain't so, Daed?" Daniel asked, worried now that Tootie suggested it.

"Only God knows what will happen next, son" John said gravely.

Emma was sitting on an old rickety chair with her head resting on her left hand. The shtruvela (stray hair) that escaped from under her prayer cap stuck to the sides of her sweaty face. Her frightened eyes stared at the havoc outside the window.

Tootie complained out loud, "I'm hot and so thirsty. I didn't get my ice tea."

"Hush up, Tootie," Nora scolded.

A flash of lightning cracked close by. An especially loud roll of thunder almost drowned out Tootie's frightened squeal. Another flash of lightning followed and a loud crack and boom.

John jumped back from the window. "I just saw that bolt hit the mulberry tree in the back yard fence line!" He pointed to somewhere behind the woodshed, chicken house and outhouse.

The storm lasted at least an hour then slowly subsided. The quiet was very noticeable when the winds died. Then sparrows began to chirp. Abraham, the rooster, crowed, trying to calm his cackling flock as they emerged from the chicken house.

"Listen, I think the storm is over," John said.

Jim agreed. "Believe so."

"Birds sing after a storm. Why shouldn't people feel as free to delight in whatever sunlight remains to them," Tootie said softly.

"Where did you get that idea?" Nora asked.

"It was something Eleanor Roosevelt said," Tootie stated.

When the Lapp family came out of the basement, they found the house intact. Outside, rain dripped from the maple tree. Under the tree were twisted and slivered branches the size of tree sprouts laying in puddles.

The sky looked threatening east of them. The storm that passed over them was still full of power as it turned the sky as black as night. John pointed out to Jim in the west, a new storm was brewing to take its place.

That same night, long after they had gone to bed, John woke up to the rumbles rolling across the sky. He went downstairs and walked out into the yard to stare through the darkness. In the not so distance west, he saw during the lightning flashes that the storm was moving toward his farm. He woke everyone up and insisted they go to the basement again. When the storm had safely passed by they went back to bed.

Chapter 8

The next morning after chores, John stuck his head in the front door. "The boys are hitching the buggy up. We should go check on the neighbors."

"Gute idea. I've been worrying about our neighbors. We can all go. They may need our help," Hal suggested.

When the women headed for the front door, Tootie trailed behind and stopped. "I think I'll stay here."

"Don't you want to see the damage the storm did?" Jim asked.

"Well, you can tell me about it later. I'll stay here and fix a meal so you can eat when you get home," she excused.

"Want to check the cow once in awhile, Aendi Tootie. She is going to have her calf soon," Noah said.

"That's what all of you told me yesterday, but all right, if that will be a help, I'll do it," Tootie said reluctantly.

An hour later, Tootie grew tired of pacing from the kitchen to the living room in the quiet house. She walked to the barn to see how the cow was doing. She was on the alert, but the turkey didn't show himself. The dog loped to meet her. Tootie scolded him as crossly as she could muster. That was all it took to get Biscuit to turn tail and hide under the courting buggy in the lean-to.

Tootie didn't know what she'd do if the cow had trouble. Birthing calves wasn't something she knew anything about, and

John certainly didn't leave her any instructions. All she was supposed to do was check on the cow. Looking at a pregnant cow couldn't be that hard to do.

Before Tootie opened the barn door, the cow let out a cranky bellow. She peeked through the crack in the door into the dim barn, hoping that there would be a pen of some sort between her and the cow. She sure didn't want to be too close to an animal so much bigger than her and so mean sounding.

No cow in sight that Tootie could see. It must be safe to enter. She eased into the barn and followed the rustle of straw bedding to one of the wooden horse stalls near the back of the barn.

Tootie gripped the wooden slats at the top of the pen and peered between them. The large black and white milk cow pawed the bedding and turned in a circle. She lowered her head and sniffed the hollowed out spot she'd made in the straw and snorted. Her nostrils flared. She lifted her head high and bellowed in pain as she doubled up with a contraction.

"Poor cow," Tootie sympathized. "You're miserable right now."

The cow made another circle with her tail cocked high. Tiny white hooves were sticking out. The cow grunted as she strained again. That contraction caused the calf's head to pop out along with a rush of bloody fluid. The cow strained one more time. The black and white calf's wet body eased slowly out.

Tootie groused, her eyes glued to the calf, "That's an awful long way to fall. Mother Nature should have thought of a softer way to get a baby cow to the ground. Please don't get hurt, baby. I'm not getting in that pen to help you with a mother as surly as yours."

Amid the bloody fluid, the calf flopped into the straw. It didn't move.

"Please breathe, baby" Tootie begged softly, her face pressed against the slats. "I don't know what to do if you don't. Please, please."

The cow licked the calf's face vigorously, mumbling

encouraging sounds deep in her throat. The baby sneezed. Its sides thumped as it took in air. The calf's head came up and wavered back and forth, slinging sticky fluid every which way. With an effort, the calf managed a squawky cry. The mother's response was to lick her baby faster and rougher.

Tootie clapped her hands in relief. "Mama, you could be more gentle. Your baby is going to be just fine. Holy buckets, am I glad that's over."

The cow's head came up at the sound of an unfamiliar human voice. When she saw Tootie, she pawed the bedding, scattering an avalanche of straw behind her that pelted the wall. Then the cow bawled threateningly.

Tootie gave a haughty sniff. "Well, I'm sorry I disturbed you. I'll leave right now."

The cow raised her head higher. At first Tootie thought she was offended. Maybe she was going to charge. No, that wasn't it. The cow was still in pain. She curled her lips up so her teeth showed and hunched her body.

"Now what are you doing?" Tootie asked wearily. "I'm ready to go back to the house. You can calm down anytime. You had the baby. If you're looking for sympathy, I'm not impressed."

The cow turned her back to Tootie. She didn't feel like considering the human staring at her. She bent double again and bellowed in misery.

"Don't tell me your problems," Tootie groused. "Start taking care of that baby so I can get out of here. This stinky barn isn't good for my allergies." She pulled a handkerchief from her slacks pocket and held it over her nose.

The cow's cocked tail raised higher. Two pink hooves came into view. The cow had another contraction.

"Oh no, another baby. Did you have to do this to me when I'm the only one home? I was just supposed to check on you. That's all everyone else was doing. Don't expect me to help you with this fix," Tootie complained, pacing back and forth. "One calf would have been enough. John would be happy with that. Why do you have to worry me like this? Stop straining right now! Suck that baby in, and wait until John gets home to do this sort of trick. You're his cow."

Another contraction, and the tiny head was out. The cow strain once more. The small calf flopped on the bedding by the other calf, disturbing the first arrival. The cow turned around, nosed the last calf and licked it.

Tootie gripped the wooden slates at the top of the pen and peered between them. Mama turned to the unsteady first calf, now on its feet, and nudged it along her side. The calf poked the cow with its nose until it found her bag. Its tail cocked up and swished back and forth rapidly as it sucked noisily. That gave the cow time to finish her wash job on the new arrival.

The second calf's head came up. It bawled a greeting to its mother. Soon it was struggling to get on its feet. In fifteen minutes, the calf was nudging the cow's other side, working its way back to her bag.

The cow closed her eyes and stood still, trying to relax after such a taxing morning. Loud sounds of both babies sucking and their tails swishing back and forth were clear signs they were enjoying the warm milk filling their stomachs.

Tootie eyes sparkled as she leaned against the pen and watched the new family. "How wonderful was that to witness the miracle of two babies born."

She'd done all she could to encourage the cow. Tootie patted her chest. She was having a little trouble breathing. Farm work tuckered her out, and she'd had enough excitement for the morning. She needed to go in and lie down for awhile. Resting always made her feel better. Then she'd start cooking. Always work to do around this place. How Nora could ever call their stay at the Lapp farm a vacation was beyond her.

Several of neighbors lost trees, but Bishop Bontrager's place next to the Lapp farm only had a few tree limbs down. Beyond Elton and Jane's farm, strips a half mile wide or more were laid bare. The funnel had taken everything in its path.

John pointed to the bare strips in Luke Yoder's woods, where mighty trees had been uprooted. "See how they fell the same direction and piled up. The tornado's strong force flattened them."

"Look right next to the downed trees, other trees and bushes were left untouched. Ain't that something?" Jim exclaimed.

A path was cut through the middle of Luke Yoder's corn field. Corn stalks looked shredded like cattle silage feed. The roof was off the Yoder barn. Twisted strips of tin lay scattered across the pasture.

Luke and his two boys, Levi and Mark, were out surveying the damage when John drove in. "Everyone all recht here?"

"Jah, we are fine. Just a mess to clean up," Luke said. "Your place all recht?"

"Jah, the tornado missed us and Elton Bontrager's farm other than some wind damage. Have you heard how the rest of the neighbors are?" John asked.

"Nah, we have not been out to see yet," Luke told him.

"We will check and let you know," John said.

Down the road, they stopped at Hamish and Edna Manwiller's farm. The couple was out in their yard, tugging at downed limbs to drag them to a pile. John opened the buggy door."How is everyone here?"

Hamish stroked his short beard nervously. "We are fine. The barn lost its lean-to and part of the tin roof, but reckon we are lucky it is not worse."

"Jah, denki to God. We will keep checking," John said. "Expect a meeting soon. We will be setting up a work schedule so you will know when a crew will be here to help you with repairs."

The Jostle barn had ended up in a pile of rubble along with three small outbuildings, including the newly remodeled chicken house. The old Hosteller house had fortunately escaped the tornado except for the loss of half the roof shingles.

The family was walking around the rubble when John drove in.

"After all that hard work to remodel the outbuildings this family has done, and now all the buildings are laying in piles of rubble. How awful for them," Hal said.

John called to Jake, "You and your family all recht?"

"Jah, we are. Lost most of our farm buildings. The animals seemed to be all recht. They are scattered all over the place. When the hen house left, it took the new laying hens with it much to my wife's sorrow."

"Sorry for your loss. We are just checking to see if everyone is all recht. Our men will get together soon, make a list of everyone's damage and help rebuild," John said.

"Much work needs done here. That is for sure," Jake agreed, looking woeful.

Emma feared the worse for and hoped for the best by the time they stopped at the Keim farm. Bobby and Adam waved at them. Adam winked at Emma as if nothing was wrong.

John asked, "How are things here?"

"Not bad, considering," Bobby said. "A few strips of tin missing from buildings and shingles from the house. Tree limbs down here and there. Will take some time to clean up."

"That is what we are hearing from everyone. Once a work schedule is made, we will be coming to help repair at the farms in the storm's path."

"Sounds gute, but we will not need as much help as others do," Bobby said. "You can put us on one of the work lists. And let us know where to go."

"Denki, Bobby. We can do that," John said as he waved his reins to start Ben moving.

The Keim brothers watched them leave. Emma kept Adam in her sight as long as she could. He was so close and so unreachable. She wished this had been a different less stressful time so she could have talked to him.

The damage report was much the same at the other farms in the tornado's path. Plenty of work to be done to reconstruct buildings and clean up but no lives lost. Everyone had made it to their safe place in time.

John stopped by Bishop Bontrager's house on the way home to report what they found. Elton said, "How soon can we gather men that were not in the storm's path to help all the others rebuild and clean up?"

"Soon I pray," John said. "Jim and I can help you put

together work groups and list the damages at each farm."

Tootie started dinner and watched out the living room window for the Lapp buggy to came in. She rushed outside to meet John. She informed him she'd taken good care of his cow. He should be really pleased, because he had two calves instead of one. She did her part. She saw to it that mother and babies were fine.

"Gute job, Aendi Tootie." John headed for the barn with Jim to see the new arrivals and check on the cow.

That afternoon, John and Jim stopped at farms not in the storm's path. Farmers were willing to help, but when they heard the name Jostle in the list they refused to help that family. Why should they care about the Jostles? The Jostle family wasn't friendly. They probably wouldn't help anyone else if circumstances were different. Maybe Jake Jostle wouldn't even appreciate their help so why bother.

John tried to change the farmers minds, but he didn't have any luck. He reported back to Elton Bontrager with the work list. It was John's opinion that the Jostle farm was one of the hardest hit. His outbuildings were all destroyed, but the farmers on the work list refused to be assigned to help Jake Jostle rebuild.

John and Jim hadn't come back by chore time. Noah glanced over the barn yard fence. The milk cows were at the far end of the pasture. "Daniel, we should go after the cows so we can start milking. It has been a long day already, and we do not know when Daed will be back. It will be gute to have the chores done."

Daniel walked through a puddle filled with tiny blue butterflies just to see them scatter. "Jah. Let's go."

The boys climbed the fence and took off across the pasture. The sun was warm on their backs. It made them thankful for the gentle breeze blowing at them.

Suddenly, Daniel grabbed Noah's arm. "Look! A little bull snake."

"So?" Noah wasn't impressed as he watched the snake, the size of a pencil, slither through the grass in front of their bare feet. He was just glad that Daniel spotted it before one of them stepped on it.

Daniel rushed at the snake and grabbed it. "Got him." He held the writhing snake up for inspection.

Noah giggled. "Jah, now what are you going to do with him?"

The snake's head curled up toward Daniel's face. "We could use a bull snake in the barn to eat mice and rats."

"That snake is too small to eat rodents. They would eat him," Noah scoffed.

"I will take care of him. He will grow." Daniel said to the snake, "Glad to meet you, Serpent. I am Daniel. He is a beauty, ain't so? Wait until the other boys see him. They will all want him."

"That snake is something all recht. As I said before, what are you going to do with him? Turn him loose in the barn now, and the cows will step on him."

"I need to find something for him to live in. I could take him to our room at night," Daniel planned.

"Emma and Mama Hal are not going to like that idea especially since we have company," Noah said dryly and marched off after the cows.

Later after chores, Daniel grabbed Noah's arm as they started into the mudroom. He pulled the snake out of his trouser pocket. "I want to put this snake in something. Quick, see what Emma has handy in the kitchen we can use to keep Serpent in."

"Sure, but you should turn the snake loose and let him take his chances. He will be less work that way," Noah hissed as he went inside. He came back with a large size, red plastic coffee can. "I poked holes in the lid with the ice pick for air," he said as he handed it to Daniel.

Daniel dropped the snake into the can, snapped the lid on and walked around the house. He set the coffee can on the front porch against the wall in the shade.

After supper and devotions were over, everyone went to the porch to enjoy the cooler evening air. John and Jim brought out extra chairs. The boys wanted to sit on the edge of the porch and dangle their legs.

Hal handed everyone a paper fan to discourage the mosquitoes that buzzed around them. As the daylight turned to dusk, a few twinkling stars dotted the sky. In the maple tree, birds twittered their good nights as one after another flitted onto the branches to roost, becoming shadowy silhouettes against the dark sky.

Emma said, "I believe I will go in and get us another bowl of that chocolate pudding while we can still see to eat it."

Handing Redbird to John, Nora said, "Sounds good. I'll help you."

Emma rowed the bowls on the table, Nora spooned the silk chocolate pudding out of the Tupperware bowl. They had to make two trips to deliver all the bowls.

Emma finished eating her pudding, retrieved the empty bowls and went back inside to get an ice cream pail of dried green beans and a mixing bowl. She sat down, put the bowl on her lap and shelled the beans.

"What are you going to do with the dried beans?" Tootie asked.

"Save them for next year's planting in the garden." When Emma finished, she said, "Now I can take the bowl back to the pantry and pour out the beans in a cake pan to dry more before I store them. The hogs will like the pods if one of you boys will empty this bowl for me so I can wash it."

Daniel took the bowl from Emma and dumped it over the hog pen fence. He brought the bowl back, went in the back door and put it in the dishpan before he came back to the porch.

In a few minutes, Emma was back at the screen door. "Hallie, did you throw away that empty coffee can I save?"

"Nah, I didn't bother it."

"Wonder what happened to it?" Emma mused.

Noah elbowed Daniel and thumbed over his shoulder at the snake's new home. Daniel nodded that he understood.

"Here's a coffee can next to my chair," Tootie said. She leaned over and picked it up. "Did you put holes in the lid, Emma?"

"Nah."

"Well, this one has a lid with holes in it," Tootie said, starting to pry the lid off.

Noah and Daniel scrambled to their feet and lurched toward Tootie. Noah cried, "Do not open the can, Aendi!"

"Too late, Tootie held the lid in one hand and studied inside the can on her lap. The elderly woman's face went pale with fright. She screamed shrilly.

"Tootie, what on earth is wrong with you?" Nora asked.

Tootie shook her head as she grabbed her chest and gasped for air. The can rolled off her lap and thudded on the porch floor, landing on its side in front of Tootie's feet.

Hal and Nora sprang up from the porch swing and rushed to Tootie. Hal said, "Take it easy, Aunt Tootie. You're all recht."

Finding it hard to breathe, Tootie rubbed her painful chest as she uttered, "S – s - snake!"

The snake slithered out and along side the can. He stopped by Tootie's foot and raised his head to stare at her. His red tongue flickered in and out of his mouth.

"Tootie, settle down. It's just a baby snake," Nora admonished, hovering over her sister.

Shaking her head emphatically, Tootie struggled off her chair with arms flailing and edge toward the screen door. Hal grabbed onto her aunt's arm as Tootie's ragged breathing caused her to clutch her chest. The elderly woman groped for the door handle. Her eyes rolled up in her head, and she went limp.

"Help me. I can't hold her," Hal cried as the elderly woman slid down the screen door.

Jim grabbed Tootie's other arm. He helped Hal lay her gently on the floor. The elderly woman's eyes were closed, and her mouth was open. She was pale and still. Her chest was barely moving.

Hal said, "She's unconscious. Give her some room to breathe. Boys, catch that snake and get it out of Aunt Tootie's sight before she comes to." She reached for Tootie's cold wrist and took her pulse. "I don't like this."

Nora's hand went to her throat in fright. "What?"

"Mom, her pulse is racing. She's having trouble breathing. I'm afraid Aunt Tootie is having a heart attack. Emma, call an ambulance and find Aunt Tootie's purse. We'll have to take it with us to the hospital for insurance information."

Nora sank to the floor to hold her sister's hand. "Tootie, wake up." Concern for her sister's condition sank in. "Hallie, her hand is so cold."

Hal said, "She's stopped breathing. Give me some room, Mom." Hal pumped up and down on Tootie's chest.

Emma hustled out of the clinic with Hal's stethoscope, a pillow and a sheet. "The ambulance will be here soon. Has she regained consciousness?"

Nora shook her head.

"Let me beside Aendi, Mammi," Emma said, taking her grandmother by the arm to help her to her feet. She spread the sheet over the lower half of Tootie's body and handed Nora the pillow. "Mammi, put the pillow under her head?"

Hal placed the stethoscope over Tootie's heart and listened. "She has a heart beat now. It's very erratic so far. That ambulance better hurry." As if summoned by Nurse Hal, in the distance, the screech of a siren grew louder as the ambulance raced toward them. "Thank God," Hal said softly.

The red, yellow and blue of the strobe lights blasted them all with color as the ambulance pulled in and braked to a stop in front of the house. The three medics Hal had worked with before, Daryl, Steve and Ivan, climbed out and brought a gurney from the back of the ambulance to the porch.

"Hi Hal, what you got going?" Daryl asked as Steve and Ivan set the gurney by Tootie.

"She's having a heart attack," Hal said.

"History of heart problems?" Steve asked.

Hal turned to Nora. "Mom, do you know?"

"I've never heard Tootie mention any problems," Nora said.

"What's her name?" Daryl asked.

"Tootie, my sister," Nora answered, staring at her sister.

"Dolly Klinefeld," Hal corrected. "But call her Tootie when

100

you talk to her.

Steve removed his stethoscope from Tootie's chest. "Her beat is erratic and pulse faint."

"I did CPR until I had her back this far," Hal told him.

"We're sending for the air-copter," Daryl said. "Minutes count."

"I agree," Hal said.

Daryl spoke in his mike. "Ambulance to dispatch."

"Dispatch," came the crackling voice.

"We need the air-copter sent to this address. We have a heart attack in progress with erratic pulse and shortness of breath. She is cyanotic and diaphoretic," Daryl said. He turned back to Hal. "How old is the patient?"

As Steve rushed past her with an oxygen canister, Hal glanced at her mother. Nora said, "Seventy-two."

"The patient is an elderly female, seventy-two years old. Is the cardiologist standing by?"

"Yes. Administer two liters of oxygen and transport," came the crackling order."

Steve slipped the oxygen cannula into Tootie's nose.

"We are administering oxygen. We will meet the air-copter at the highway intersection with this gravel road. Send fire department out to block off the road," Daryl ordered.

"Will do," the dispatcher said.

Steve laid a gurney blanket on the porch floor by Tootie. Ivan collapsed the gurney and helped Steve rolled Tootie enough to get the blanket under her. The three medics lifted Tootie and scooted her onto the gurney. They eased the gurney down the steps and rolled it to the ambulance. In seconds, the ambulance rushed on its way, blaring the siren.

"Let's go to the hospital, Mom," Hal said.

Jim said, "Get in our car. I'll drive."

Hal turned to the others. "Emma, you take care of the girls. It's their bedtime. We will be back as soon as we can."

Chapter 9

After the ambulance left, Daniel sat in Tootie's chair and leaned over with his elbows on his legs and his head in his hands.

Emma patted Beth on the back to keep her from crying as she turned on him angrily. "Daniel, how did that snake get in my coffee can while the lid was on it?"

Daniel straightened up. "It is only a small bull snake I caught to put in the barn. I wanted something to keep it in until the snake grows a little more. I did not know you were saving the coffee can."

"Next time ask," Emma said sharply.

Daniel was beside himself. His lips quivered. "Aendi Tootie is sick, and it is all my fault. I did not mean to cause her to have a heart attack. If only she had not opened the can. Noah and I tried to stop her, but we were too late. Serpent would not hurt her. He is just a baby."

Noah added, "Aendi, did not know Serpent would not harm her."

John said, "Serpent? You named that snake already."

Daniel opened the can and held the snake up with two fingers so they could get a good look at the writhing serpent not much bigger than a large nightcrawler. "He is a beauty, ain't so?"

John frowned at the snake. "If you say so, Daniel."

"Well, I do not think so," Emma said, with her hands fisted on her hips. "What are you going to do with that snake now?"

"I am going to keep him," Daniel said. He put the snake back in the can and snapped on the lid.

"Where? He cannot stay in that coffee can for long," Emma demanded.

"Do you want your can back?" Daniel asked wearily.

"Nah, I do not want that dirty can back now," declared Emma. "I just want to know where you are going to keep that snake?"

"I am going to turn him loose in the barn," Daniel floundered. "I thought the snake would be gute to have in the barn to eat mice when he is bigger."

Emma proclaimed, "You cannot turn that snake loose now. You have to keep it contained until after my wedding. Tell him, Daed. I will not have him disrupt my wedding with another creature like he did when you and Hallie married."

Noah nodded toward his brother as he defended, "Daniel was a small child then. He is grown up enough to know he cannot disrupt his sister's wedding in that way again."

"I know Bishop Bontrager would not be happy with me for sure," Daniel said, remembering the lecture he received from the bishop after the frog incident at his father's wedding. Wondering why Emma was making so much fuss, he stared at her and repeated, "I just wanted the snake for the barn. I will keep the coffee can in the barn where it will be far away from the house. Do not worry. The snake will not be big enough to turn loose for a long time yet."

By the time Jim drove onto the highway, the air-copter was far in the distance headed to Wickenburg hospital. They had the road to themselves as Hal gave her father directions to the hospital.

When Hal led the way through the automatic doors, Lucy Steinford, dressed in green scrubs, greeted them briskly. "Hi, Hal. The air-copter patient yours."

"Yes. Matter of fact, she's my aunt."

103

"Sorry to hear that," Lucy said soberly.

Hal turned toward her parents. "Lucy Steinford, this is my parents, Jim and Nora Lindstrom from Titonka, Iowa. Dolly Klinefeld is Mom's sister."

"Sorry your sister isn't well, Mrs. Lindstrom. I need to fill out the admittance papers. Can you help with that?"

"Of course," Nora said, opening up Tootie's large handbag. She moved the Amish book out of the way and found the billfold.

It seemed forever before Lucy had all her questions answered. She copied Tootie's insurance cards and handed them back to Nora. She pointed behind them to an open door. "Take a seat in the waiting room. They're working on Mrs. Klinefeld now in an ER room. A doctor will be out as soon as he can to talk to you."

Jim turned on the television. He grumbled that the late night shows hadn't been the same since Johnny Carson retired, and turned the remote control off.

Nora hands trembled as she picked up a Good Housekeeping magazine. She flipped through the pages and inspected the cover. "For pity sakes, this magazine is a year old."

Hal watched out the door, feeling apprehensive about her aunt. She wished she could be in the ER room with Tootie like she was with other patients she brought in.

She glanced at her mother when Nora tossed the magazine back on the pile. Her mother needed to get her mind off how bad Tootie might be. "Mom, after what happened, Aunt Tootie is never going to come back to see us again. I just know it."

Nora gave her daughter a weak smile. "Oh, I think she will. Of course, she might bring a list of rules next time instead of that silly Amish book." Nora patted Tootie's purse in her lap and gave Hal a weak smile. "I can name them now. Such as no pet snake, no calf watches and all turkeys and dogs penned up."

Hal tried to smile as she looked out the waiting room door. Watching the ER exam rooms brought her close to tears. "Mom, I'm so sorry this happened to her."

Nora grabbed Hal's hand and squeezed it. "Now, now, dear. At our age anything can happen, and Tootie has not taken very good care of herself. Take a deep breath and calm down. I think you said it best when you said Aunt Tootie is Aunt Tootie. How do any of us know how she's going to react to any given moment? See a tiny, harmless snake and have a heart attack. That was a bit dramatic for even Tootie."

"Mom, please. This is serious," Hal declared.

Nora nodded solemnly. "How well I know it is, and I'm worried about her, too."

An hour later, Dr. Stan Christensen, his stethoscope draped around his neck over his green scrubs, came to the door. Hal greeted him and introduced her parents.

With serious blue eyes, he told them, "Mrs. Klinefeld is stable now. The EMT had to use the defibrillator on her in the ambulance to bring her back. Now that she is stable, the cardiologist wants to watch her for awhile before we move her to a room. She's going to spend the night here for observation to make sure her heart stays in rhythm. Tomorrow I want to run some tests before I release her. Hal, has your aunt mention not feeling well?"

"No. My mother is Tootie's sister. We talked about it on the way here, and none of us had noticed anything. She has complained of tiredness lately, but we thought Aunt Tootie was just being Aunt Tootie."

The doctor gave her a questioning look.

"Never mind. You would have to know my aunt to understand. What happened tonight set off my aunt's heart attack. Tootie opened up a coffee can and found a small snake in it that one of my sons caught. She became very frightened, had a hard time breathing, grabbed her chest and passed out."

"I see," Dr. Christensen said. "Well, you folks might as well go home and get some rest. I should know more by noon tomorrow when the test results are in. If anything comes up before then, we'll call you at home. Otherwise, I imagine Mrs. Klinefeld can go home tomorrow afternoon."

"Thank you, Doctor," Nora said. "Can we see Tootie?"

105

"I wouldn't advise it. She's very groggy right now. Going in and out of sleep. Probably wouldn't even know you're with her. Anyway, she needs the rest. You can peek in at the door if you want."

"Yes, that would be good enough," Nora said.

Nurse Lucy said, "I'll show you where your sister is."

The next day, Hal left with her parents to go to the hospital right after lunch. Once the doctor released Tootie, with instructions to come back the next week for a check up, they headed home.

Jim and Nora helped Tootie climb the porch steps. She greeted John and his kids lined up to welcome her as she went into the house. Everyone trailed along behind and stood in the middle of the clinic, watching Nora and Hal help Tootie into bed.

When Hal and Nora stepped out of the way, Tootie looked at the long faces around her. "Holy buckets! I'm not dying yet. Stop looking so worried, will you? I just need a nap before supper, and I'll be good as new."

"Aendi Tootie, you are eating supper in bed tonight," Emma informed her.

"I can make it to the table. You shouldn't go to the bother to wait on me with all you have to do," Tootie objected.

"Let Emma and the rest of us pamper you for awhile, Aunt Tootie. You can get up tomorrow as long as you take it easy," Hal said. "Now we'll get out of here and let you rest."

Noah and Daniel started for the door. John laid his hand gently on Daniel's shoulder. "Not so fast, Daniel. You tell Aendi Tootie you are sorry for scaring her."

As Daniel eased closer to the bed, his eyes moistened. He reached for her hand and patted it. "Aendi Tootie, I am sorry for upsetting you. I do not want you mad at me. I did not know you were going to open the coffee can and see the snake. I am sorry you do not like snakes."

"I understand that. Boys will be boys. You're forgiven." Tootie waved her other hand toward him. "But I hope you won't let that creature get loose around me again."

"Nah, the coffee can is in the barn. It is going to stay there," Daniel assured her.

"Go on now, and don't give this another thought. Tomorrow I'll be as good as new." Tootie waited for Daniel to leave before she said, "John, don't be hard on that boy. He didn't mean any harm."

"He is harder on himself than I am on him. He does feel really bad that his snake scared you," John said. "Now you rest. I reckon Jim and I should get at the milking."

Tootie yawned. "This has been a very trying two day for me. Coming face to face with that snake was awful. Then all those tests today. I think I can take that nap now."

Hal kissed her gently on the forehead. "You do that, Aunt Tootie."

Late in the night, Hal woke up and immediately thought about her aunt. She slipped out of bed and picked up her flashlight from the floor by the head of the bed. It wouldn't hurt to check on Tootie.

She eased down the stairs and over to the clinic door. She could hear Tootie's rumbling snores. The elderly woman was able to sleep. That was a good sign. When Hal peeked in the room, she saw a figure hunched over on a chair by the bed.

Hal slipped across the room and laid her hand on Daniel's shoulder to wake him. He straightened up on the chair, rubbed his eyes and blinked at her. Hal whispered, "You can go to bed if you want. Aunt Tootie is sleeping. She's all recht."

"I feel better staying by Aendi Tootie to help her if she needs something," Daniel whispered.

Tootie's snores stopped. She said huskily, "Hallie, I told Daniel a couple hours ago to go on to bed, but he's still here."

Daniel took her hand. "I want to be here if you need anything."

"That's nice, dear, but I won't need anything tonight." Tootie teased, "You will be all worn out tomorrow when I will expect your help. Believe me, I'll think of all sorts of things in the morning you can do for me if that will make you happy. Now go get some rest. Both of you."

"If you are sure. I feel like your being sick is all my fault, and I wish I could make it up to you," Daniel said dolefully.

"That's nonsense," Tootie declared. "We didn't know I'd get that scared. That's what I get for being a nosy old woman. I shouldn't have opened that coffee can. Believe me, I've learned my lesson. That's the last can I open while I'm around you boys. No telling what I'd find in the next one."

That made Daniel giggled.

"Good night, you two. Go to bed so this old lady can rest," Tootie ordered.

For several days, Daniel stuck to Tootie like a cocklebur. One morning, she said she felt well enough to venture out. "Daniel, could you hook up one of the buggies and take me for a ride?"

"Jah, recht away," Daniel said, turning to leave. He whirled back around. "Which buggy?"

"It doesn't matter really. Which buggy do you prefer."

"The courting buggy?"

Tootie smiled. "That's a good choice for what I have in mind. I'd like to go for a ride in it. That buggy will do fine."

Nora frowned. "Are you sure you're up to riding in a buggy?"

"Yes, I feel like getting some fresh air. I do feel so much better this morning. Besides, I'm running out of things for Daniel to do for me here. Maybe a ride would make him feel like he's done enough," Tootie assured her.

Where are you going?" Nora asked.

"Just for a ride with Daniel," Tootie replied mysteriously. "There's something I should have done before now. For a day or two, I thought I might not ever get the chance. Best take care of that errand before it is too late."

When Tootie picked up the bouquet of silk white lilies from the clinic room table, Hal and Nora had their answer.

As Tootie walked to the buggy, she took a deep breath. "Such a lovely morning."

"Jah, that is recht. Did you have some place in mind to go?" Daniel asked as he eyed the flowers.

"I guess I better run an errand I had planned while I'm still able walk. For a while I thought these flowers were going to have to be for me," Tootie said pragmatically. "The cemetery is where we're headed. This bouquet is for Peter Rogies. Think you can help me find his grave?"

"Jah, I can," Daniel said solemnly. He put his hand under Tootie's arm and helped her into the buggy.

As they left the driveway, Tootie said, "I don't remember how to find the cemetery."

"Jah, I have been there many times. I know the way."

"I thought you might." Tootie watched the countryside as Daniel let Mike take his time. "The fields and pastures are so pretty this time of year. This is a nice ride. You're doing it just right, Daniel. Slow and easy."

"Jah, but Mike is doing the all the work," Daniel said, grinning at her.

"You know it's fitting we're taking the flowers to Peter in the courting buggy. He really liked this buggy a lot," Tootie said, remembering the time Peter took her for a ride down Bender Creek road on a dark night without asking Jim if they could use the buggy.

"Why are you taking flowers to Peter?"

"I liked him very much. We were friends, and I miss him especially when I'm visiting his neighborhood," Tootie answered. "Is it all right with you that I visit his grave and leave him flowers?"

Daniel looked thoughtful. "Jah, I think everyone when they pass on should have someone remember them once in awhile and leave flowers. As long as we are going, I wish I had some flowers to take to my mother."

Tootie studied the bouquet of white lilies on her lap. "Daniel, how about I share with you? This is a big bouquet. You can break a couple flowers off for your mother. I don't think Peter would mind sharing his flowers for a good cause. Think that would do?"

Daniel smiled. "Jah, Aendi Tootie. That would do gute."

"I know these silk flowers last longer, but I see so many

109

pretty wild flowers along the road sides. They will do if you ever get the notion to go to the cemetery again by yourself."

"That is a gute idea, Aendi Tootie. I will remember," Daniel said solemnly.

Chapter 10

The next morning, John and Jim went back to the Bontrager farm to talk to the bishop again. John asked, "Have you made a decision on what to do to get the others to help Jake Jostle?"

Elton said, "We can start on this end of the storm damage and work our way down the road. Maybe when we get to the Jostle place I will be able to change the men's minds."

By the time the workers stopped for Sunday worship service, the next farm to work at was Hamish Manwiller. The Jostle farm was a neighboring farm to Manwiller and Keim's.

The worship service was at the Bontrager farm. The bishop noticed the Jostle family wasn't greeted or spoken to by many of the members. This unfriendliness had gone on long enough. Soon the Jostle family would decide to quit coming to services. Bishop Bontrager had to find a way to change the minds of the men in his congregation.

The service began with the hymn *The Old Rugged Cross*. After that hymn finished, Bishop Bontrager asked John Lapp to be the next song leader for *Lob Lied*. That song was the long one that gave the ministers time to discuss what they wanted to preach about that morning.

The bishop took Preacher Yoder and Deacon Yutzy upstairs to a bedroom. The bishop said, "I have given today's service much thought. What I want to happen is the three of us unite to awaken an understanding in our congregation so we do not have a repeat of what has happened lately. This shunning of the

Jostles had gone on long enough. They need to be made feel they are wilcom in this community. Jake Jostle's farm is on the list to repair soon. His farm was one of the hardest hit. He needs help. We need to help him and his sons rebuild and be glad by the grace of God we are able to do so."

Preacher Luke Yoder said, "I agree."

Deacon Yutzy nodded.

So the three clergymen came back downstairs and took their seats. The hymn ended. Deacon Yutzy stood before the congregation and lead off by reading scripture from Colossians. "Therefore, as God's chosen people, holy and dearly loved, clothe yourselves with compassion, kindness, humility, gentleness and patience. Bear with each other and forgive one another if any of you has a grievance against someone. Forgive as the Lord forgave you. And over all these virtues put on love, which binds them all together in perfect unity."

The deacon sat down, and Luke Yoder gave a sermon on how grateful they all should be to God that no lives were lost in the storm. It was a blessing that they were a giving community that looked out for each other and were willing to help their neighbors rebuild."

Next was Bishop Bontrager's turn. He preached, "The Bible says, A merry heart doeth gute like a medicine. I know how much all of you appreciate humor. After the destructive storm we just suffered, we need reasons to make us laugh.

I have a parable to tell you. I hope it makes you laugh or at least smile. I am telling you this parable to help you understand what is the recht thing to do when we all feel we have a tough decision to make. It is important to help each other like we have all week with our clean up efforts. We need each other at times like these. When the need arises I do not ever want you to think it is not your concern when something bad happens to the other fellow. We are all going to need help at some point in our lives and will appreciate that help.

Now let me tell you about a mouse that lived in a farm house. He watched the farmer and his wife through a hole he gnawed in the wall baseboard.

One day, he saw the farmer and his wife open a package they received in the mailbox.

"What gute food might this contain that I might sample?" The mouse wondered.

The mouse stared as the farmer reached into the box and brought what was in it up to look at. The mouse was devastated to discover it was a mousetrap.

Retreating to the barn yard as fast as he could, the mouse proclaimed a warning to the red hen as she scratched in the scattered hay for weed seeds, "There is a mousetrap in the house!"

The chicken clucked and continued to scratch in the dirt. The mouse didn't leave. She could see he was waiting for a reply so she raised her head to speak, "Mr. Mouse, I can tell this is a grave concern to you, but it is of no consequence to me. That mouse trap is not going to hurt me out here in the barn yard. It is your problem to solve. I have food to find. I cannot be bothered by what worries you."

The mouse turned and saw the pig root by the fence. He ran to the pig and told him, "There is a mousetrap in the house!"

The pig sympathized, "I am so very sorry to hear that, Mr. Mouse, but there is nothing I can do about it but pray for your safety. You be very careful from now on. Be assured you are in my prayers."

The cow was grazing in her grassy pen. The mouse turned to her for help. "There is a mousetrap in the house!"

The cow said, "How terrible, Mr. Mouse. I'm sorry for you, but that news means nothing to me. It is your problem."

So the mouse scurried back to the house, head down and dejected. He had to face the farmer's mousetrap alone.

That very night, a sound was heard throughout the house as the mousetrap snapped, catching its prey. The farmer's wife rushed from her bed to see what she caught. In the darkness, she did not see it was a venomous copperhead that had slipped in under the screen door. His tail was all the trap caught. Before she could back away from him, the snake bit the farmer's wife on the leg. The farmer rushed her to the hospital, and she returned home with a fever. The farmer put her to bed. Everyone knows you treat a fever with fresh chicken soup. Recht? So the farmer took his hatchet to the barn yard for the soup's main ingredient. He butchered the nice, red laying hen. Remember, she said the mouse's problem was of no consequence to her.

The farmer's wife's sickness continued to worsen as the snake's poison spread through her system. Friends and neighbors came to sit with her around the clock. To feed them, the farmer butchered the pig. Remember the pig refused to do no more than pray for the mouse.

When the farmer's wife died, many people came for her funeral. The farmer had the cow slaughtered to provide enough meat for a lunch for all of them. Remember the cow told Mr. Mouse that the danger was his problem. Not hers.

The mouse looked upon all that happened to his barn yard neighbors from his hole in the wall baseboard with great sadness. "If only my neighbors had helped me get rid of the mousetrap the loss of their lives could have been prevented."

Bishop Bontrager shook his finger at everyone in the room. "The moral to this story is very clear. The next time you hear someone is facing a problem, and you think it doesn't concern you, remember, when one of us is threatened, we are all at risk. We are all involved together in this journey called life. We must keep an eye out for one another and make an extra effort to encourage one another to do the recht things by our neighbors. An example is how we lend a hand to help each other. Such as recht now when the tornado caused so much damage. Each of us is a vital thread in other people's life tapestry."

After Bishop Bontrager sat down, Preacher Yoder stood up. He added to the bishop's parable. "Sind unser hend voll bluth? Can you recall any other time your hands were covered with blood, because you would not help another human being in his time of need?"

Members of the congregation nodded no.

"Gute, then think now before you refuse that help to another person in this community that needs of our help. Kneel to pray about this and say a word to God for all these families that had damage done to their farms. We are not done yet, lending our aid to others. Some still need our help and prayers through this coming week and maybe the next one after that. We need to do God's biding and help them."

After lunch was served, Emma went looking for Adam. She caught up with him just in time. He had hitched Sophie up to the buggy.

"Adam Keim, you stop recht where you are. I want to talk to you before you leave," Emma hissed.

Adam looked puzzled. He pulled his notepad out of his pocket and wrote, "I was just coming to find you. I want to show you something. Want to come for a ride with me?"

"Nah, you go for a walk with me," Emma commanded.

Adam nodded and started down the driveway.

Emma grabbed his arm. "Not that way. Everyone can see us. We're going behind Jane's chicken house where we can talk in private."

Adam smiled, thinking pleasant thoughts about what would happen when he was out of sight with her.

Once they were behind the chicken house, Emma took a deep breath and turned to face him. "I want to know what is going on with you, and I want to know recht now."

Adam seemed surprised by her angry tone as he shrugged.

"Do not play dumb with me. Did your mother tell you I have been worried about you?"

Adam nodded yes. He wavered his hand in a question.

"Want me to give you some reasons why I am worried?"

Adam nodded yes.

Emma eyed him critically. "Why is it really that for weeks you have stayed as far away from me as you can? I am thinking it is not because of a lot of work like everyone tells me including you. That never stopped you from calling on me before. Do you want to marry me or not?"

Adam expression revealed nothing as he nodded yes.

"You are very sure you are not trying to find a way to back out? Maybe you just do not have the nerve to say so to my face?" Emma accused.

Adam nodded a slow no. He wrote on his pad, "I have been very busy."

Emma lifted her chin and hid her trembling hands in the deep folds of her skirt. "I am glad you have a successful business. Did Priscilla tell you I stopped by the shop?"

Adam nodded yes, leveling a penetrating gaze on her.

"Tell me why our apartment has not been worked on over the shop. You cannot possibly get the work done now before the wedding. Where do you expect us to live if you plan to marry me?"

"I have that solved. Do not worry," Adam wrote.

"Worry is all I do lately. You are never around anymore. I cannot talk to you to find out what problem is solved and what isn't. That is enough to make me worry about all sorts of things. Ideas that I do not want in my head are tumbling around in there, and I have not been able to talk to you," Emma complained.

Adam's face wore a patience look as he wrote, "I am sorry I worried you."

"You should be. Does it not matter to you that I miss you being with me most of all. That I would worry about you when I have not seen you for days? Do you realize that?"

Adam watched her for a long minute, his expression unreadable. Finally, he nodded yes.

"Gute! Now are you sure you want to marry me? After all, Priscilla gets to see you more than I have in weeks," Emma said.

Adam straightened up away from the building with a scowl as he scribbled quickly, "What does Priscilla have to do with anything?"

"She is a constant source of temptation. It is very clear that Bobby cannot resist her. Maybe you cannot, either, now that you see her every day," Emma accused as she stared into his eyes, sparking with anger.

116

Adam shook his head slowly as if he didn't believe what he heard come out of Emma's mouth.

Emma stomped her foot and raised her voice. "I am serious."

Adam studied her for a long minute. He could see she meant the accusation. His face flushed fiery red as he wrote, "You wait until now after all these years we have been together to tell me you do not trust me to love only you. You think I am the kind of man that says he will marry you and back out because of another woman without telling you." He thrust the note at her.

Emma read it. "I do not want to think those things. No matter what is wrong between us, I want to hear the truth from you."

"I did not realize there was anything wrong between us. If you do not think any more of my trust and love than this, you better make up your mind if you want me for a husband. You give more thought to what kind of man you think I really am. If I am as bad as you think, you are the one who should call the wedding off. I am going home. You know where to find me. You make up your mind what you want to do, and come let me know. I WILL NOT COME TO YOU." Adam slapped the note into her hand. His back was stiff with anger as he stalked off.

Emma read through her tears the blurred message. She slid down the chicken house wall to the ground and wiped the tears on her face with her sleeve. She hadn't ever seen Adam this angry before. She didn't think she'd ever be able to erase the wounded look on his face from her memory. That was enough to make her realize she might have been wrong about Adam's faithfulness to her

What had she just done? Bishop Bontrager was right. She was a doubting Thomas. She expected Adam to prove he loved her, and that he was faithful to her. Why hadn't she just believed in him? As hurt as Adam was now, he may never forgive her. She was destine to be a maidel, and it was all her fault.

Emma dried her eyes on her skirt hem and stood up. She wanted to get past the house and curl up in the enclosed buggy away from everyone. She knew she looked terrible with puffy eyes and tear streaked face, and she just couldn't face questions now.

Later that afternoon, the family gathered at the buggy to leave. They were surprised to see Emma already seated inside.

Hal said, "We wondered where you were."

Emma looked out the back window to avoid Hal's gaze. "I did not feel gute, so I laid down on the seat for awhile."

"What seems to be wrong?" Hal asked, feeling her forehead.

"I just need to rest for awhile," Emma said wearily.

When supper was ready, Hal went to Emma's room to check on her. Emma said she didn't feel well enough to come down for supper. Hal offered to bring up a plate of food, but Emma said she wasn't hungry.

Hal could see Emma didn't have any physical symptoms of an illness. However, something was diffidently wrong with her.

The next morning, Bishop Bontrager instructed one of crews to go with him to the Jostle farm to work. The men didn't balked at the idea. When they got there, Jake greeted them. They shook hands with him and went to work along side Jake and his boys, rebuilding the blown down structures.

That evening at supper, John and Jim told the women that the bishop's sermon really helped. Jim talked about how great it was that the Amish men banded together to help the strange family without complaining. When John checked on their progress later in the day, he said the men were talking to Jake like they had always been friendly with him. What they didn't get done by evening, the men told Jake they would be back to finish the next day.

John said, "The buildings are smaller than the old ones, but they will do for the Jostle family to get them started again."

"That is a cute, little chicken house. Now all Mrs. Jostle needs is some more chickens to put in it," Jim added.

Emma perked up. "I can give her a crate of mine to get her started."

"That would be great," John told her.

Tootie said, "How far that little candle throws his beam so shines a good deed in a weary world."

Nora's head went back. "Where did that come from?"

Tootie replied to her sister as if Nora should have known. "Don't you ever read William Shakespeare?"

The next few days, Emma moped. She didn't speak much while she worked. Finally one morning, Hal could see Emma was upset enough she wasn't going to get over whatever it was, and she was past the point of just missing Adam.

Emma dried the plates and put them in the cupboard. She dried the kettles, stacked them and placed them on top the plates. Hal waited until Emma's back was turned and put the kettles in the pan cupboard.

Hal handed Emma the scrap pail to empty to the cats in the barn. Emma dumped it in front of the chicken house. She left the pail in the chicken yard and came back empty handed.

Hal put a kettle of vegetable soup on the back of the cookstove to simmer. She asked Emma to get her the salt box. Emma brought her the pepper container.

Hal decided she'd waited long enough for the girl's disposition to change. She took the paring knife away from Emma and handed it to her mother. "Mom, you finish peeling the apples. Emma and I are going for a walk."

Emma started to shake her head no.

"Jah, recht now," Hal said sternly, pointing at the back door. She didn't mean to sound as if she was ordering a child around, even though Emma had acted like one for some time now.

Hal was content to walk in silence down the lane until they were away from the house. She looked back to make sure they were far enough away. "Spill it. What's bothering you?"

"I do not want to talk about it," Emma grumbled, focusing on the turning pumpkins in the vine covered patch at the edge of the cornfield to avoid looking at Hal.

"Your father told me Sunday afternoon Adam come from behind Jane Bontrager's chicken house without you. He was really upset. Left right away your father said. I take it the two of you had a disagreement."

"Sort of."

"Is that anything like being sort of pregnant? I didn't want to butt in, but Adam hasn't been back to make up. So I'm asking. I might be able to help if you explain what happened. Keep in mind you only have a few weeks until the wedding. This is not a gute time to stay mad at each other."

"There may not be a wedding." Emma snapped, watching her bare feet.

Hal stepped in front of Emma and grabbed her by the shoulders to make her stop walking. "Look at me. What are you telling me?"

"As mad as Adam is at me, he is not going to marry me," Emma moaned.

"You didn't think your family needed to know the wedding is off. We have worked hard to prepare a nice wedding for you two," Hal scolded.

"Ach! I did not know what to do," cried Emma. "I kept hoping Adam might cool down before I had to say the wedding was off."

"All recht, why is Adam that mad at you?"

Emma took a deep breath and studied Hal with tear filled eyes. "Remember when I talked to Bishop Bontrager about my worries, because I didn't see Adam anymore."

"Jah, and that didn't help?"

Emma nodded her head sideways. "The bishop did not have any sympathy for me. I told you he called me a doubting Thomas. I never really understood why the bishop said that even though he explained the bible verses to me. Not until yesterday anyway, after I cornered Adam behind the chicken house. I opened my big mouth and stuck both feet into it. By the time I realized I had done the wrong thing, it was too late."

Hal looked very stern. "Fudge! What did you say?"

"I accused Adam of not wanting to marry me. I said that was why he stays away. Not because he is so busy working. I accused him of hiring Priscilla, because he likes her more than he should and wanted her around every day."

"Fudge! How awful for that sweet man. Emma you should be ashamed of yourself," Hal scolded.

Emma's shoulders sagged. "I am now that it is too late."

"You go to Adam recht away. Tell him you're sorry."

"I cannot do that. He told me I needed to take time to think about what I accused him of. If I did not trust him any better that that, we should not get married. He said it was up to me to find him and tell him I did not want to marry him."

"All recht, you have thought about this and know what you want so go to him."

Emma shook her head. "It has probably not been long enough to let Adam cool down. You did not see how hurt and angry he was."

"I can imagine. I'm glad I didn't see him after you ran him through the wringer. What are you going to do now? You do want to marry Adam, don't you?"

"Jah, I do. I love Adam. Still, I do not know what has been wrong with him. He has acted strange all summer. First, I cannot catch up to him to talk to him so I worried. That is when all sorts of bad thoughts came to me. Adam did not answer me when I accused him of trying to get out of marrying me. I still do not know if I am recht or wrong about some of the things I said to him."

"It seems really strange to me that after Adam and you have been so close for so long that his feelings would change over night. Don't you think that would be unlikely to happen?"

Emma's lips flattened together as she thought. "Jah, it does not seem like the Adam I know and love."

"Sure, now if you really trust him you need to tell him you were wrong. Ask him to forgive you. Sooner or later, Adam will give you the answers you want when he isn't mad at you anymore. The most likely one is he has been busy all summer as he said, working to build a nest egg for the two of you. How sad it is that you'd accuse that hard working man of doing something untrustworthy. He adores you."

"Ach, that does make sense when you say it. I just cannot go see him yet. Adam was so angry he does not want to see or talk to me now." Emma sniffed, trying not to cry.

"Well, give him a little time to cool off. That may help some, but keep in mind, you don't have much time left. When he starts missing you and realizes the wedding date is soon, maybe he'll come talk to you."

Emma shook her head. "Nah, Adam is not coming back. I tell you, you should have seen his face. It turned to red stone. He scratched his last words in big capital letters. "I will not come to you."

"So you go to him. I'd say you should have to after what you accused Adam of doing. Swallow that pride for the sake of the man you love. If you remember, I had to come face your father and talk to him to get him to marry me after I turned down his marriage proposal. If I could do that, you can, too."

Emma said sullenly, "That was different."

"Nah, it wasn't that much different. Your father wouldn't confide in me about what had taken place in your family, concerning your mother. That bothered me. I told him I wouldn't marry him if he kept secrets from me. I thought I meant that. Then I missed him so much. I knew I loved him, and I knew the gentle, caring man your father was. I wanted to spend the rest of my life with him.

So I came here to tell your father I'd marry him without knowing the family secrets. Do you think it was easy for me to swallow my pride and face your father with that admission? Nah, but I had to do it, because it was the recht thing to do for your father and me.

With a little encouragement from you, John told me what happened to your mother, before he married me even though he no longer had to tell me. So you see there is probably a happy ending for Adam and you, because you love each other. It is up to you to make it happen, Emma, by showing him you really trust him no matter what awful things you were thinking and said to him."

"I have to think about this," Emma said as she turned around at the hayfield and headed back to the house.

The next morning after kitchen clean up, the women had a

second cup of coffee while they discussed their plans for the day.

Nora said, "Emma, has there been any change with Adam?"

"Nah."

"Mom, I told her she's going to have to trust him with the same blind faith we have in our husbands," Hal said.

"Yes, I agree."

Emma snapped, "You both are so sure of your faith in your husbands. Did you know they lied to you not once but twice recently?"

"Holy buckets!" Tootie exclaimed, her eyes wide.

"Emma!" Hal snapped, setting her cup down hard. "You shouldn't talk about your father and grandfather like that."

Nora looked shocked. "What makes you say a thing like that?"

"At the quilting frolic, I mentioned to Roseanna Nisely that Samuel must be glad his hay was made with help from our men. She said I was mistaken. Samuel had not made his hay yet. Daed said that was where they were going, and they were gone all day."

"I see," Nora said slowly.

"But, ...," Hal began.

"John and Jim are as honest as the day is long," Tootie interrupted to defend them.

Emma held her hand up for them to listen. "Again at the quilting frolic, I asked Joe Fitzmiller if he had a gute day at the salebarn, talking to Daed and the others. He said he did not see them. They did not come to the salebarn. Why did Daed lie both times? They were gone all day that day, too, so where were they?"

"Emma, your father always has the best of intentions. If he didn't want us to know what they were doing, I'm not going to get upset," Hal said and glanced at her mother for confirmation.

"Absolutely, I feel the same way. I have faith in both men. We will find out what they were up to one of these days. Whatever they did is nothing to worry about," Nora agreed.

123

"Sure, if you say so," Emma said doubtfully. "I just wished I could say the same about me and Adam."

After lunch, Nora asked Jim if they could go for a ride in his courting buggy. Jim was surprised that his wife volunteered but pleased just the same.

Later that afternoon, Nora came back with a smile on her face. She caught Hal alone in the kitchen and whispered, "I was right, Hallie. The men had a good reason for not telling us where they were when they disappeared for two days."

"What was the reason?"

"I can't tell you."

"Oh, Mom! Not you, too," Hal groused.

"I promised your father not to say anything. John will have to tell you if he thinks he can. The men kept still, because Adam wanted them to let him tell Emma in his own time."

"If Adam and Emma's attitude doesn't change soon that may never happen. We will never know what he was up to all summer," Hal complained unhappily.

The number of days before the wedding were fading away, and no sign of Adam. Soon it would be time for the wedding to be published at the worship service. Emma couldn't let that happen until she knew there was going to be a wedding.

One night after everyone was in bed, Hal told John the problem between Adam and Emma had gone on long enough. "Something has to be done to get them back together. Emma is so miserable."

"Adam has got to be as miserable as Emma. He thinks the world of that girl or did," John defended.

"John, could you go talk to Adam for Emma? Get him to come see her?"

"Nah, and you are not doing that, either. This is between them and none of our business. We should not interfere. If they cannot solve their differences now, they would not be able to live a gute married life together as man and wife."

"Then will you at least talk to Emma? See if you can get her to swallow her pride and go see Adam. That's what he said he would be waiting for," Hal said.

"I think we should leave what happens up to them, but I can talk to Emma if you think it would help. She mopes like a motherless calf, and I cannot stand to see her so unhappy."

"Gute, I knew I could count on you," Hal said.

After Emma tossed and turned for half the night, she got out of bed and slipped downstairs. The house was hot. Maybe the cooler night air would help. It certainly couldn't hurt.

She eased open the screen door. The cool porch floor felt good to her bare feet. She sank down on the edge of the porch.

Out of no where, Biscuit showed up. He nosed her hand, asking to be patted. She rubbed the top of his head. The satisfied dog flopped down beside her. He put his head on his stretched out front legs and closed his eyes. In the distance, the Bontrager dog barked. Biscuit's head jerked up, his ears perked to alert. He wrinkled his nose like a rabbit, sniffing the air.

Emma patted his head. "Relax. That dog is not close."

In the dim light of a quarter moon, Emma leaned back against the porch post, trying to take the advice she just gave the dog. She took a gulp of fresh night air and filled her lungs. The freshness only served to make her more alert.

A quiet time like this was soothing to the nerves. Just what she needed. Clouds were banking up from the east. Tomorrow was bound to be cloudy with a promise of rain that wouldn't happen.

Behind the house, the windmill creaked out a soft whine in the gentle breeze. Emma listened for movement at the barn. She wondered if cows and horses ever had a restless night like people.

She could make out the ghostly movement of a creature by the road ditch. She squinted through the darkness and recognized Buttercat, prowling in search of a mouse.

An owl hooted somewhere in the distance, probably roosting in the picnic grove. That was a pleasant sound to fill the silent spot in this night when she felt so miserable.

Soon the calmness of the evening blanketed Emma. Her head nodded uncontrollably. She was ready to go back to her room and get into bed. No way did she want to fall asleep beside Biscuit on the porch, and have someone in the family find her there in the morning.

Chapter 11

Morning came too soon for Emma after the restless night. She hated to get out of bed. After breakfast, while the other women cleaned the kitchen, Emma left with the scrap pail swinging back and forth in her hand.

The soft clop of hooves caused her to stop at the edge of the driveway. The sun overhead was bright in her eyes so she squinted and tried to make out who drove in. She was hoping against hope it would be Adam.

With dread, she realized it was Priscilla Tefertiller's fiberglass buggy. That was the last person in this world she wanted to see this morning. Priscilla stopped her horse close by Emma and climbed over the seat. She stalked toward Emma.

"Wilcom," Emma said coolly.

Priscilla halted in front of her. "I have something to say, and I expect you to listen." Emma's mouth flew open. Priscilla didn't give her a chance to reply, and the frost in her voice would have frozen over Bender Creek. "Adam tells me your problem is you think he has an interest in me even though you know that I am going out with Bobby. That does not make sense. I am here to tell you that you are wrong.

I like my job, and because of you, I am in danger of losing it." Priscilla lifted her hand to stop Emma's response. "I am not through talking yet. Adam says he might have to let me go if you come back to him. I need my job, and you are not being fair to me, trying to get me fired when I have done nothing wrong. You need to stop torturing Adam. Make up with him so you can get married. Adam has suffered long enough already. That is all I have to say."

Priscilla climbed back in the fiberglass buggy. Emma watched dust flog behind the buggy as Priscilla's horse did a pretty good clip down the road. Emma had to chew on the shame Priscilla's fast, angry words brought her and try to digest them without getting sick at her stomach.

Emma wanted to get away from the house for awhile. She'd go for a walk. Get off by herself so she could think about how much she cared for Adam, and how she'd wronged Priscilla and Adam. Bobby must be upset with her, too. No doubt since Priscilla is mad, she told Bobby what was bothering her.

Emma didn't want Priscilla to lose her job. Adam needed a sales clerk. She sure didn't want the job. If Adam married her, she wanted to teach school. How had she messed things up so badly?

Emma's surroundings didn't register as she shuffled in the lane, putting one foot in front of the other one. When she came to the hay field, she realized she was at the end of the lane. She'd gotten there too soon. She didn't want to turn around and go back to the house yet.

In front of her was the pasture gate. She climbed over the gate. The walnut grove was across the pasture ahead of her. That quiet spot was dense enough to hide in and perfect to be alone. She trudged through the dew sprinkled grass and stepped around the cow piles.

Hazy vapor shifted across the pond top and hovered over the draw, adding a surreal atmosphere.

Mourning doves cooed to each other. Emma usually liked to hear their calls, but today the doves sounded as doleful as she felt. A dove flew down and landed in the cow path ahead of her. Emma saw the soft gray-brown bird strut toward her. She stopped and waited. The bird got within a few feet of Emma and stopped to preen its feathers. At first, Emma wondered at this wild bird's assertiveness. Then she remember something her mother once said about a mourning dove coming close was a sign of impending grief. Emma clapped her hands. The disturbed dove chortled as it flew away. Emma watched the bird disappear and prayed silently that nothing worse than what she was suffering came her way. She had to leave it in God's hands that he had better things planned for her than the dove did.

Emma reached the tree grove and walked out of the sun into the cool shade. The sun couldn't find too many holes in the leaf canopy to poke through so the picnic area was dimly lit with shafts of light spearing the grass in spots.

The darkness matches my mood, Emma thought.

She knelt in front of the wooden crosses partially hidden by tall grass and pulled grass around her mother's cross so she could see it better. As Emma flopped down with her back against a walnut tree, she said to the cross, "Mama, why did you have to die? You could have stayed around long enough to help me solve my problems." She thought for a moment about the past and said sorrowfully, "Reckon you had enough problems of your own, ain't so? You did not even try to solve your own."

Mindlessly, Emma waved at mosquitoes that dotted the air around her face. She watched the birds flit from tree to tree and wondered what it felt like to have their freedom. A squirrel chattered nervously. Somewhere, a pheasant crowed and another one answered.

This was just what she needed. She was so tired from fretting and lack of sleep. She hadn't had a good night's rest in weeks. Emma closed her eyes and leaned her head back against the tree just to relax for a moment. Her eye lids grew heavy, and she dozed off.

Later, Hal searched for Emma. She wasn't in her bedroom. It was almost lunch time, and she hadn't seen Emma since early morning. Hal stepped out on the porch. Emma wasn't working in the garden. The scrap pail was at the edge of the front yard. Hal went after it. The scraps were still in it. Emma hadn't emptied it. Now she was really concerned for Emma. She spotted Noah and Daniel coming out of the barn. "Is Emma with you?"

"Nah," Noah said.

Daniel pointed at the lane. "I saw her walk that way after she talked to Priscilla Tefertiller."

"Priscilla was here?"

"Jah, I could not hear what Priscilla said, but she sounded mad," Daniel said.

"Have you seen your daed?" Hal asked urgently.

"He is in the barn with Dawdi. They are working on one of the milk pipelines," Noah said. "Why? What is wrong with Emma?"

Hal hurried past them and stepped into the barn. She didn't notice the boys stayed right behind her. "John?"

"Recht here," he called as he came from the milk room. "Was ist letz?

"Emma has been missing all morning. Daniel says he saw her walking down the lane after Priscilla Tefertiller talked to her. They must have had an argument. Emma was going to empty the scrap pail. She didn't do that, and she didn't come back to the house. I can't find her anywhere. I'm very worried about her."

"Why is she that upset?" Noah asked.

Daniel's face turned white. "Would she go near the pond?"

"Of course not," Hal said, rubbing Daniel's back. "Adam and Emma had a disagreement. She's upset because of it. That's all."

"I will find her." John gave a deep sigh and studied Hal. "I guess this is the time to have that talk with her, ain't so?"

"Jah. Try the picnic grove. She likes it there," Hal suggested.

"Jim, I have to go see about Emma. I will be back soon," John said.

"You do what you have to do. I can finish this problem with a little help from those two tall lads beside you," Jim said, winking at the boys.

John made quick strides as he hurried across the pasture. Once inside the grove, he glanced around and found Emma.

130

Her chin was resting on her chest. He sat down next to her and patted her arm gently.

Emma woke with a start.

"Sorry, I did not mean to scare you."

"That is all recht, Daed. I should not sleep during the day. What time is it?"

"Close to noon." Emma looked so frazzled. John's heart went out to her. He hoped he said the right words to help comfort her.

Emma started to stand up. "Ach, I need to get back to the house and help Hallie."

"Not just yet. Hal and Nora have dinner ready. Hal sent me to find you to tell you to come eat, but first she wanted me to talk to you."

"About what?"

"Hal told me what happened between you and Adam. It is time you talked to Adam. You cannot put it off any longer. The time to announce is coming Sunday next at the service. We have to know one way or the other if the deacon is to announce your wedding for the 15th. If not then, you would have to wait another month.

This problem between you and Adam is making you sick. I am sure Adam is miserable, too. You are letting this problem gnaw on you like a dog on a bone. Worry is not solving a thing. Take my advice and face Adam. Swallow that unholy pride of yours and take your medicine," John said frankly.

"What will I say that will change how hurt Adam is?"

"You did not just hurt his feelings. You took away his unshakable belief that you trusted him no matter what."

Uncertainty showed on Emma's face. "If I only knew what Adam did all the time he stayed away, the argument would not have happened. He could have told me so I would not worry, ain't so?"

"Maybe, but you got angry and accused him of harsh things that were not true. Adam was not going to tell you what you wanted to know after that. You have to start practicing to be a submissive wife." John rubbed a sideburn. "Truthfully, I think that is going to be hard for you do. You have never been the submissive one around here. Go to Adam in blind faith now if you really want to spend your life with that man. You tell him you trust him, and you ask his forgiveness. As hard as it is going to be for you, you wait until he is ready to confide in you the answers you want."

"Ach! That is going to be so hard to do," Emma declared.

"You do want to marry Adam and spend the rest of your life with him, ain't so?"

Without hesitation, Emma said softly, "Jah."

"My girl, go to Adam. The recht words will come. Remember, this time be submissive like you should. Try to keep your words soft and sweet so you do not have to eat them again another time."

"Knowing Adam, I will not get another time. He may not even believe me this time," Emma said.

"Then you pray that you say the recht things to Adam and hope he is willing to take you back.

I think Adam can understand you are nervous about leaving the only home you have known. That thought makes you edgy. Tell Adam that. He will understand, but, Emma, you are ready to leave the nest. Go make a life for yourself and have a family of your own. We will manage fine without you. Hal will be all recht if that is what worries you."

"Is that what you really believe?"

"Ach, the boys and me will be here to help her when she needs us."

"Have you put it to Hallie that way?"

"Nah," John said slowly. "I do not want to put doubts in Hal's head or get her upset with me for thinking she might need help. Emma, in that way, you are more like Hal than you are your mother. Submissiveness has always been hard for Hal. If I remember recht, she mentioned that would be her weakness when we talked about marriage. Besides, I know you will not be far away if she needs you." John smiled and patted Emma's knee.

"It is gute to know you can get along without me. I do worry about how Hallie will manage the household by herself. Jah, I will come help any time you want me." Emma paused then asked, "You just said I will not be living too far away. Do you know where I will be living?"

John smiled and said evasively. "With Adam. Now that is all you are getting out of me. I best go back to the house for dinner. Come when you get ready."

After he left, Emma rose to her knees and folded her hands together. "God, Denki for sending Daed to tell me that the family will be able to manage without me. It is gute to know I have one less worry. Now can you please help me figure out what to do and say to make Adam forgive me? Put the recht words in my mouth. Give Adam the patience and understanding to forgive me and continue to love me. Amen."

The next day, Emma announced after kitchen cleanup she would be gone for part of the morning. She was going to see Adam.

"Oh, gute!" Hal exclaimed.

"We're proud of you for finally working on your problem, and I'm sure Adam is waiting for you," Nora said.

"Good luck, dear" Tootie added.

Priscilla was washing windows when Emma parked by the shop. She glanced over her shoulder as Emma asked, "Is Adam here?"

Priscilla swiped vigorously at a stubborn fly speck. "Ach, jah, he's been in that shop every day lately, moping more than working."

"I need to talk to him."

Priscilla jabbed at Emma's back in a needle sharp tone. "You most certainly do. It is about time."

Emma walked along the aisle between the furniture in the shop and knocked on the workshop door. "Adam, it is Emma." She opened the door. Adam kept sanding on a wooden dining room chair without looking up. "Is is all recht that I come in?"

Adam gave her a quick, disinterested shrug with one shoulder.

"We need to ... ." She licked her lips and started over softly,

133

remembering her father's warning about swallowing her pride. "I need to talk to you." Adam didn't acknowledge her. She pushed on. "You said I had to come to you so here I am." Adam kept sanding. "I thought about what I should say to you long and hard before I came to talk to you. The least you can do is pay attention while I talk." Her voice grew weary and faded out as she stared at his back.

Daed said she had to keep her tone soft. She couldn't be assertive or bossy sounding. It might work on her father and her brothers but not the man she planned to marry. Especially not when he was so mad at her.

Emma breathed easier when Adam turned the sander off and placed it on the chair seat. With ridged jaws, he moved to the table. Once he eased onto the table top, he folded his arms over his chest and crossed his legs at the ankles. She had his attention, but his eyes were too observant without expression. There wasn't a sign of what he was thinking.

Usually so good at reading his mind, Emma couldn't this time. She was as nervous as a flighty chicken spooked by a hovering hawk. Adam certainly wasn't making it any easier for her. She felt as though she was in the bishop's hot seat. Understandably, she sensed that was how Adam wanted her to feel. He was hurt, and he wanted her to know it. Whatever happened was up to her. She had to bring her scattered thoughts together in her head. She'd have to say what Adam wanted to hear if she had a chance of convincing him she loved him.

Emma gripped her trembling hands tightly together in front of her so Adam wouldn't see how much she was shaking. "I was wrong to talk to you the way I did. I should not have said those awful things. I knew better the minute the words were out of my mouth when I saw the hurt on your face.

I do have faith in you and in us. I do trust you, and I want to marry you. I want to grow old with you." She couldn't take his blank stare much longer. Maybe if she moved around she'd managed to get through this moment.

She paced at the end of the table while she rambled on, glancing at Adam now and then to see if there was a change in his demeanor. "What you saw and heard that day was not the Emma I am. I think after all these years down deep you know that. I could not change so completely in such a short time.

Hallie says I have always been the one to hold my family together. I have taken care of them since I was very young. Sensible, dependable Emma, that is me. I always saw everything so clearly and took care of what needed to be done. That was me. You have been around my family enough to know that. Even after Daed married Hallie, I had to keep the household running smoothly.

Somehow lately, I lost sight of the real Emma, the sensible, take charge one. I have been nervous about leaving the only home I know. I worried my family still needs me. All the wedding plans have been thrown at me for approval, and you weren't there to help me make the decisions. Hallie needs advice on everything, including something as simple as whether to open two cans of corn or one.

With the company around, I have not had a moment's peace. Even Mammi and Aendi Tootie's harmless squabbling has gotten the best of my nerves. I needed quiet space to think. There was not any time or place for that.

I wanted to talk to you about all this. You would understand. You have always been my rock. I could count on you to help me feel like I can make it through the wedding fuss. Except, you were not there. I have not talked to you for days. I missed you so much I came up with all sorts of crazy ideas about why you stayed away. Everyone kept telling me you were busy. Busy doing what? Working, they said. At what? You could tell me when you talked to me, they said. I needed you recht then not some far off time.

It has taken me awhile to come to my senses. Everyone has stood up for you when I complained. They told me to trust you to do the recht thing. They made me ashamed of the way I have acted. They helped me see how much I hurt you by accusing you of things that were not true.

I am still full of butterflies about starting a new life with you. I still worry about how Hallie will handle taking care of

Daed and the kids without me. Daed says they will be fine. He says he can always come get me if they need help.

I have to believe that is so, because most of all, I really want a home of my own with you and our children. The fear of never seeing you again is making me sick inside. Knowing I caused you so much hurt is a burden I will never forgive myself for.

I am so hard to live with Hallie and Daed are ready to throw me out of the house soon. Even if you do not forgive me.

I came to tell you I will not make the same mistake twice. I will not hurt you again by mistrusting you. If only you can find it in your heart to forgive me."

She stopped pacing and glanced at Adam. He was still watching her with that expressionless look. A sinking feeling, like a lead weight on a fish line dropping to the bottom of the pond, tightened in her gut.

Emma wondered if he was trying to figure out if he could believe her or not. She could understand he didn't want to go through this heartache another time. She couldn't blame him if he didn't want to put up with her. She had it coming, but she wished he'd hurry up and make up his mind one way or the other. She needed put out of her misery. "Ach! I know. I'm talking too much without giving you a chance to say anything."

Adam shrugged.

"Do not give me that answer. I know there is a whole lot of words in your head that no one but you can hear. So tell me what you are thinking. Are you going to give me another chance or not?" Adam didn't move. She couldn't take much more. She was running out of words and courage.

She was tired beyond description and growing irritation was mounting in her. Her feisty self took over. Submissiveness and the gentle words advice from her father were quickly forgotten. She put her hands on her hips. "Adam Keim, there is no one more important in this world than you are to me. I love you. I want to spend my life with you if you still want me. Would you rather I get down on my knees and ask your forgiveness in front of God, the bishop and everyone at the Sunday service next? I am desperate enough to do that."

A brief flicker of amusement gleamed in Adam's eyes. He shook his head no.

Emma's brow furrowed in exasperation. She didn't know what else to say. "All recht! Get your bottom off that English customer's table top. Come here, and tell me what you want me to say or do to make it recht between us."

Adam slipped to the floor and stopped in front of her. There was a beleaguered expression on his face as he took her in his arms and hugged her tightly.

In a small voice and trying to be hopeful, Emma asked, "Does this mean you are not mad at me anymore?"

She felt Adam's head move sideways as he nodded no.

She stepped back. "Ach, Adam. What do you want me to do?"

Adam nodded toward the shop.

Emma hesitated a moment, trying to read his mind. "Ach, you want me to go talk to Priscilla."

Adam wrote, "Apologize to her. If she accepts you are sorry, I will forget this disagreement. Do that if you really want to marry me."

"Being your wife is what I want. It is what I dreamed of for the last three years. I have not changed my mind."

With a stubborn look on his face, Adam pointed again at the open door.

Emma walked into the shop with Adam behind her. He intended to stand behind her, listening to every word to make sure she said what he wanted to hear. She prayed silently all the way across the room. She hoped she sounded convincing enough to please Adam. She didn't care much what Priscilla thought. Emma really found it hard to like her.

Priscilla glanced over her shoulder at Adam and Emma and kept washing an already clean window.

"May I talk to you?" Emma asked contritely, clasping her hands in front of her.

"Sure." Priscilla's voice was indifferent. She wasn't going to make this easy.

Adam stepped around Emma, put his hand over Priscilla's

hand to stop the swiping motions. He turned her around to face Emma. The wet cloth dripped on the floor around her tennis shoes as he pointed to Emma and cupped a hand over his ear.

"All recht, Adam, if you say so. What do you want, Emma?"

"To say I am sorry. I knew better than to think that Adam loved anyone other than me. I was just searching for reasons he was not coming to see me. I was upset with him. Saying what I did was my way of getting back at him. It was a mean thing to do to both of you.

I know how much you mean to Bobby. That is why the spiteful thoughts I had did not even make sense to me. I want you to know how sorry I am for upsetting you. Adam needs your help here at the shop, and I want you to work here if you want this job."

Priscilla looked at Adam.

He nodded agreement.

"Sure, Emma, I will accept your apology and forgive you if Adam wants me to do that. I want Adam to be happy." She spoke like the words burned her throat. When she focused on Adam, she said gently, "I want to stay and work for you. I do like this job."

Chapter 12

On Sunday meeting day, a week and a half before the wedding, Preacher Bontrager stood after the final hymn. "If the Lord wills and we live, in two weeks the worship service will be held at the Kenneth Swartzendruber farm.

There is not a member meeting this Sunday and no disciplining needed." With twinkling eyes, he looked at John Lapp and stated, "We have the first marriage of the season to announce today. Deacon Yutzy can come forward and publish the details."

Deacon Yutzy read from a piece of paper, "I have a die hoctzich dawk announcement. The first marriage for the season will be John and Hallie Lapp's daughter, Emma Lapp, to Lovina Keim and the late Elmo Keim's son, Adam Keim."

The deacon asked John to stand and offer the details. John said, "The wedding is at the Lapp farm on September 15th. Everyone here is invited."

John sat down, and Bishop Bontrager announced, "This service is adjourned for this Sunday. It is time for lunch and fellowship."

There was much talk in the kitchen about Emma's wedding. Women volunteered to help with preparations. Emma had her hands full delegating jobs.

The following Monday, Adam picked up Emma, they went to the county seat to get their marriage license. Adam was back to his old self as if nothing had happened between them.

What Adam knew about where they were going to live after they married, he was not sharing with Emma. She still had questions, but she wasn't going to ask and risk making Adam mad.

Three days before September 15th, wedding frenzy began. Early that morning, two buggies pulled up by the house at the same time, Hal exclaimed, "Beth and Amy to the rescue just like they did when John and I got married."

"Who is that?" Tootie asked, standing behind Hal at the kitchen window.

"John's sisters. Come meet them," Hal said, heading for the door.

As the two women came up the porch steps, their black hair showed through their black prayer caps. They had dark brown eyes like John. There was no doubt they were related to him.

"We're so glad you came to help today, Beth and Amy," greeted Hal.

Emma laughed as she hugged the women. "I'm afraid you have your work cut out for you helping to right this house."

Beth, slim and wiry, shook hands with Nora and Tootie as Hal introduced them. "We would not have missed helping for anything in the world. Would we, Amy?"

"Ach, nah!" said Amy, a plumper, shorter version of her sister. She stood on tiptoes to hug Hal and Emma. She patted Hal on the back as she said, "It is gute to see Emma so happy."

"We all agree," Hal said.

"Boy, do we agree," Tootie said with meaning. Beth and Amy smiled politely at Tootie as Nora elbowed her sister.

"Schwestern Hal, find us the wash pails for the window cleaning. We will start with that," Beth said, running a finger down the living room window. As she left a trail in the dust, she said, "You agree, Schwestern Amy?"

"Jah, but keep the broom handy so we can tackle inside the house next."

"Emma will go get what you need," Hal said. "Mom, Aunt Tootie and I need to finish in the kitchen and get prepared for lunch."

Tootie and Nora were just about done with the breakfast dishes. Hal was mixing up a white cake when a commotion broke loose in the living room.

Redbird's shrill voice screamed, "Dam, Dam!"

Beth echoed, "Dam, Dam."

The front screen door slammed.

"What on earth?" Nora exclaimed.

Hal was mystified. "Where did they learn cuss words?"

Nora held her flushed cheeks. "What must John's sisters think of those two little girls?"

Tootie stopped drying her hands on Emma's dish towel and stared down both women. "Don't either one of you look at me! That is not something I would say."

Emma giggled as she looked out the window. "It is all recht, Aendi Tootie. It is not your fault. The girls just saw Adam drive in. I think they are trying to say his name. Now they have wrapped themselves around his legs. Adam is caught for sure. He cannot walk."

Hal gusted a sigh of relief. "We better go get them and work on the correct pronunciation of his name before they greet him at a worship service. I'd hate to hear how Stella Strutt would twist her story about me as a mother if she heard Redbird and Beth cussing."

John and Jim came from the barn to greet Adam. Noah and Daniel followed along behind, giggling behind their hands.

Jim chuckled. "I'd say those two little girls are excited to see that guy."

"Overly excited from the sound of things," John said dryly.

Adam knelt between the girls. Redbird knocked his straw hat off and rubbed the top of his head. "Dam, Dam."

Beth smiled as she patted his cheek. "My Dam."

"Nah! My Dam," Redbird retorted.

Adam put a finger to their lips and shook his head, trying to look stern, but they weren't buying it.

"Wilcom, Adam," John said.

Adam nodded and tried to smile as Redbird put a choke hold on his neck. "My Dam."

"You here for all day?" Jim asked.

Adam tried to nod yes.

Jim chuckled. "Good! Maybe those two will ease up on you before the day is over."

Adam grinned.

When Hal came out on the porch, Beth and Amy were laughing so hard, she thought they were going to fall off their stepladders. Hal scolded playfully, "Fine aunts you two are. Don't encourage those girls. It's hard enough to make them mind." She rushed to Adam's rescue with Emma following behind her. "We'll save you, Adam."

Adam gave each girl a hug and let the women pick them up. The girls protested loudly, waving their hands at Adam for help, shouting, "Dam, Dam!"

John rubbed his beard and eyed his laughing sisters. "Hal, we need to work on what is proper to say when the girls greet people."

"Jah, but John, Emma thinks they're trying to say Adam's name. We just need to get them to pronounce his name correctly," Hal assured him.

"It is gute to know that they have not picked up such rough words from somewhere," John said, his lips twitching at the corners. "Adam, come to the barn and hide with us. We are close to done."

"Yeah, it might be a good idea for you to get out of sight for awhile until those two calm down," Jim added. "They were roughing you up but good."

Trudging along with them, Adam rubbed his red neck.

As soon as milking equipment was cleaned, the men met with the women in the kitchen.

Adam looked cautiously around the room as soon as he walked in.

Emma giggled and said softly, "You are safe for now. The girls are playing with their dolls in the living room."

The men sit down at the table with Tootie. John set up the plans for the hog butcher the next morning while Nora poured each of them a cup of coffee. "Usually we kill the hogs when the weather is cold, but we are not going to be working up this hog except into pieces that will fit in large pots. The women cook the meat and pull it off the bone. I have rented a refrigerated trailer that will park on the yard in the morning. All the food will be stored in it."

"I sure know about winter butchering. When I was a kid, Dad sent me to spread the word to my uncles, Dad's two brothers, to bring their families and a hog to butcher. We all shared the meat, because we butchered three or four hogs. That was hours of work, but sure good eating that winter," Jim reminisced. "What are we going to do today?"

"We get a barrel and one of the large, cast iron kettles out of the shed. Noah and Daniel, it will be your job to fill the kettle. The water has to heat early in the morning. That is your job to light the fire. You stack wood under the kettle and a large pile nearby to feed the fire until the water is hot."

"The women will get all the large pots and pans ready for the hog meat. As we cut it up, they can get the meat on the stove to cook. Jim, Adam and me will check out the chin up poles."

"Now what might that be?" Jim asked.

"It is the frame work behind the chicken house that we hang the hog from to work on it. Over time, some of the poles are not study. They rot. We need to go to the timber this morning and cut as many limbs as we need into large stout poles."

"To answer your question, Dawdi, Daniel and I use the framework to do chin ups sometimes," Noah said.

"I see," Jim exclaimed. "Well, John, send these two boys out to do a few chin up and see how the frame holds up."

John grinned. "That is a gute idea. Try it, boys. While we are in the timber, we have to pick out some small pieces of wood and whittle sharp points on each end. They will fit in the hog's hind legs."

Aunt Tootie leaned back in her chair and patted her chest. "Holy buckets! What happens next?"

"Tootie, watch what you say!" Snapped Nora. "We have big enough ears playing in the living room."

"Sorry," Tootie said sheepishly. "It's just that I missed out on

143

the way meat was prepared when I was a kid. This is interesting to me. So go on. I want to hear."

John explained, "After the hog has been dipped up and down in the boiling water to scald it, the stobs suspend the carcass from the cross pole so we can scrape the hair off. The scolding hot water loosens the hog hair. With this gute help, we will get done fast." John grinned at Jim and Adam. "Hope you are ready for the lifting. The hog is a heavy one." He smiled at Emma. "I've been saving the largest one for this wedding.

Noah, you and Daniel dig out one of the log chains we use to pull the hog up and down in the water. Lay it by the kettle. Emma, get out the knives and see if they need sharpened. Have them and the whetstones laid handy for in the morning. Hal, Nora and Aendi Tootie can get all the pots and pans ready for us to lay the pieces in as we cut the hog up."

The next day after chores, John went in the house and got his rifle to shoot the hog. Adam, Jim and the boys walked with him to the pen.

Tootie asked, "What is John going to do with the gun?"

Emma answered, "That is what he uses to kill the hog."

"Holy buckets! He shoots the poor thing," Tootie cried.

Nora said, "How on earth do you think they get the hog to cooperate when they're cutting him into pieces?"

"I didn't think about that part at all," Tootie said.

"Aunt Tootie, sit down," Hal said, placing a cup of coffee on the table. "Brace yourself, and it will be over with in a minute. I know just how you feel. I felt the same way when I saw Emma butcher chickens for the first time."

As the men looked over the fence, Jim asked, "Which one is it?"

"The black one with that white ring around his neck," John pointed out. "I have to wait for him to turn around and look at me. Can't stir hogs up. Meat will be tough if we do."

The hog quit rooting dirt and turned to look in the direction of the voices. John raised the rifle to his shoulder and pulled the trigger. The hog fell and kicked for a few minutes. That caused the other hogs to squeal and kick up a cloud of dust as they rushed to the far end of the pen. They turned to stare at the fallen hog. When the men entered the pen, they snorted and squealed in fright as they smelled blood.

As quick as they could, John and Jim tied a rope around the hog's front legs. Adam and the boys wrapped their hands around the rope and helped pull the animal from the pen into the grass. Jim handed John a knife to cut the hog's throat. Blood ran from the slit as the hog's heart finished beating. They rolled the hog onto a homemade sled. All of them took hold of the rope and dragged the sled behind the chicken house where the work was to be done.

A fire blazed under the steaming kettle. The water was boiling. John and Jim hooked up the log chain to the hog. John threw the chain over the top post of the chin up structure. They all grabbed the chain to started pulling the hog up and down into the water. As soon as the steaming hog was ready, Noah went for water to douse the fire under the kettle. They scraped off all the hair, leaving the skin exposed.

When that was done, John cut the hog open all the way down the front to remove the entrails. The guts fell into a metal bushel grain basket.

There was much laughing and joking as the men sawed and cut the hog into pieces. Nora and Tootie were busy in the house, cooking lunch. After Hal and Emma had been outside for awhile, washing loose hairs off pieces of meat, Nora said, "Tootie, take one of the smaller pans and go get the liver so we can cook it for lunch."

Tootie stepped out the back door. "Nora wants the liver now." Hal and Emma turned to her. Their clothes were splattered with big splotches of blood. Emma reached into a kettle of water and brought the dark blob up in her hands. Stained water dripped off it, speckling the ground and their bare feet red.

Tootie grew wide eyed as she backed up to lean against the house wall and screamed. All work stopped. The men turned to see what was wrong with her, their knife points poised toward the sky. Amy and Beth jumped off the ladders and ran around the house.

Nora raced outside, letting the mud room door slam behind her. "What on earth is wrong with you, Tootie?"

Tootie pointed a wavering finger. "Hallie and Emma are hurt. See! They are all bloody."

"Aendi Tootie, it is just butchering day," Emma said simply.

"There's nothing to worry about," Hal said. "Not a pretty sight I know, but it's got to be done. We always look this way. Was there something you wanted, Aunt Tootie?"

"I got to sit down." Tootie thrust the pan into Nora's hands and disappeared inside. Nora held the pan out to Hal. Her face quivered as she tried not to laugh "I'll take the liver in, please."

Emma put the liver in Nora's pan as Hal said, "Remember that list of don't dos if we want Aunt Tootie to come back to visit again. We can add she is not helping with hog butchering."

"Is your aunt going to all recht?" Beth asked Hal.

"Jah, we're used to this. Aunt Tootie recovers quickly," Hal said, giggling.

"You are sure she will not have another heart attack?" Amy asked.

Nora stuck the liver pan on her hip as she said, "I'll go check on my sister just to make sure."

As soon as the meat was rinsed off, Hal and Emma made several trips to pick up pans filled with leg pieces, shanks, shoulders and hams, before the chickens or the cats could sneak in and steal a bite. Nora and Hal put the chucks in large kettles already filled with steaming water.

As soon the meal was ready, the men stopped to rest and eat. Amy and Beth put down their brooms and came to the table. The dinner consisted of brown beans, turnip greens, mashed potatoes, fried liver, cornbread along with plenty of fresh churned butter, milk and coffee. Dessert was a blackberry cobbler and whip cream.

After lunch, the men went back to butchering. They removed the spine, the tenderloin, from the carcass. The rest of the body was cut into two sides of back and two side of front.

Jim used a meat saw to cut the top off the head and removed the brain to be fried with scrambled eggs for supper. Emma was ready with a bowl when he scooped the brains out of the skull and dropped them into her pan.

The boys emptied the dirty water out of the black kettle, and Hal cleaned it. "When you are ready you can pour the fat chunks into the kettle now," she said.

"Got them ready and waiting," Jim told her. He dumped two large kettles of fat cubes and gave Hal the kettles to wash.

The fat rendered into lard in the kettle over the open fire. It was a hot job. Hotter in warm weather than on a cold winter day. So the women took turns stirring the fat chunks constantly to keep it from burning. Tootie even offered to take a short turn.

In the kitchen, Hal ladled the melted fat into a lard press so she could squeeze all the lard out, leaving small, hard pieces of meat and skin in the press. She dumped those pieces on baking sheets.

Tootie's nose wrinkled up as she watched. "You keeping that?"

"Jah. We call those cracklings. We put a handful of them in bread or just eat a handful like that for a snack."

"Oh," Tootie said in a tiny voice.

Emma said, "Lard cake is gute with cracklings in it. When we have time we should mix a cake up for you."

"Oh, goody," Tootie said dryly. She sat at the table while the women worked on the meal. Hal looked around at Tootie with the thought Tootie could set the table to be a help. Hal watched her aunt while she cracked the eggs in the skillet of brains. Tootie looked tired. She'd had a busy and long day. Hal decided not to ask her to set the table. Best let her rest. They shouldn't expect too much out of the woman. After all, she just had a heart attack.

Hal smiled when she thought of Tootie's reaction to hog butchering. The elderly woman was probably wondering why she had gotten so excited over hog butchering yesterday. She wouldn't want to see another hog cut up any time soon.

Later, as the bowls passed around the table that evening, Tootie said, "Oh, good, I love scrambled eggs."

"Tootie, maybe you shouldn't take any," Nora said, putting a hand over her sister's on the spoon.

"I am, too, taking some." Tootie sounded argumentative.

Nora gave up. "Fine then. Take some and pass the bowl on."

Later, Jim said, "Pass the fried brains back around. They were good. Haven't had any hog brains in ages."

Tootie's face scrunched up as she looked around the table. "Which bowl were they in?"

Nora said, "The one next to you with the scrambled eggs in it."

Looking queasy, Tootie said, "You put brains in with the scrambled eggs! Why didn't you tell me that, Nora?"

Nora giggled. "I tried to, but you wouldn't let me. They must have been good. You cleaned up what you put on your plate."

Tootie gave her plate a hard look. "I wondered what the soft, white chunky stuff was in the eggs. I thought it was thicker than usual egg whites."

"That was brains, and good fresh ones," Jim said.

"You ate them." Nora narrow her eyes at Tootie, daring her to make a fuss.

Tootie picked the bowl up and holding it at arm's length gave it to Nora to pass on to Jim. "Hallie, just so I know, did you cook all the brains, or will there be more in scrambled eggs for another meal?" Tootie asked.

"That was all of the brains for this butchering," Hal answered.

"Good," Tootie said softly.

"So what did you think of butchering day now that you have been here for one?" Adam wrote, smiling at her as he handed her the note.

Tootie read the note out loud. "Adam, yesterday I was excited about being here for the butchering. I thought I'd like helping with it. Truthfully, today not so much."

Chapter 13

The day before the wedding, men came to unload the bench wagon. They moved the living room and clinic furniture to the basement. The divider wall between the clinic and living room was opened. They carried the benches in and set them in rows with an aisle down the middle. In front of the benches were the chairs for the ministers and the wedding party.

While that was going on, other men put up a large tent in the yard for the reception. They brought in tables and benches, placed side by side in the shape of a U. As the tables were completed, a woman placed white tablecloths on them. The corner table, the *eck*, was reserved for the bridal party.

Workers carried in large chests filled with breakable dishes and eating utensils. These chests were used for large crowds at weddings and funeral meals. Several men in the community had the responsibility for storing the chests at their house and renting them out for an occasion.

The day of the wedding started early. The whole family was up at four o'clock. In fact, they managed to beat Abraham's first crows by a good ten minutes.

Noah offered, "Emma, I will feed the hens this morning."

"Gute, but do not let them out. I do not want chickens under foot. For sure, who knows how Tom Turkey would react to so many strangers being here for hours," Emma said with a sigh.

By six, the helpers started arriving. The three hostlers, Emma's former students, stood by the barn to take the buggies.

Jimmie Miller, a yellow haired boy, had sprouted up as fast as Daniel. Matthew Stoll, the school trouble maker that Emma grew fond of by the end of her first term, and Mark Yoder, Levi's younger brother were the other two hostlers.

The boys considered being a hostler a big honor. They drove the buggies out in the hay field and parked them in three rows. The horses were tied to a rope stretched taut between two hay wagons. The hostlers biggest job was to feed and water all those horses at midday.

The guests didn't leave at the same time. The driver of each buggy had to walk to the hay field and match up his horse to his buggy. Invited English and Mennonite guests parked their cars in a line by the barn.

By seven, Adam, Emma and their attendants had eaten breakfast and changed into their wedding clothes. They went out to the tent and took their place on a bench near the opening.

The two male attendants had Adam between them, and Emma sat between her attendants.

The waiting line of buggies grew long as guests waited for the hostlers to take their buggies. As far as could be seen from both directions on the road, buggies were starting up, moving forward and stopping.

People walked across the yard to get in the reception line. The bride, groom and their attendants greeted the guests and shook hands with each of them. The women went into the tent to visit, and the men congregated by the house to wait. The children gathered on one side of the house and the teenagers on the other side.

As Noah and Daniel strolled across the yard, Jimmie Miller called, "Guder mariye."

"Guder mariye. You fellows will have your work cut out for you today," Noah said. "This promises to be a big wedding."

"We know it, and we will do our best," Jimmie assured Noah on his way to the next buggy.

Finally, it looked like the last of the guests had arrived. The crowd stood around, waiting.

Noah said to Daniel, "Time we get into the greeting line.

Promptly at eight thirty, the forgehers (ushers) escorted the ministers into the house to the three chairs that faced the wedding guests and the bridal party chairs. Bishop Elton Bontrager, Minister Luke Yoder and Deacon Enos Yutzy, sat down, waiting to start their three hour wedding service and ceremony.

The relatives of the bride and groom went inside. Well wishers gathered to the side in groups to wait their turn to be taken in by the ushers.

People were seated by age and relationship to the bride and groom. The women sat on the left and the men on the right like at Sunday service. Young relatives came in next so the ushers motioned for Daniel and his cousins to come with them.

Next were the couples recently married or had published their intention in church to marry soon. The couples came in and separated to their respective sections. Cousins and friends concluded the procession of guests.

This fine morning, the better portion of the district's congregation had made it a point to gather to witness this wedding. John Lapp was a well respected member of the community, and his once English now Amish wife, Nurse Hal, was a valued addition. So many of the guests could tell stories about how she helped them and probably would before the day was over.

As for the bride and groom, Emma was an excellent teacher. Parents felt lucky to have her teach their children. Adam was a highly liked young man with a prospering furniture business. He sold to both Amish and English customers.

Two empty benches left at the back were for the helpers to sit on when they had a moment to get away from the kitchen. Other helpers listened in the kitchen as they quietly worked.

The men left their hats on the shelves in the bench wagons. Removal of hats signified that the house was now a place of worship. The ministers kept their hats on until the first song was over which was according to an old custom.

Bishop Bontrager stood and announced the opening of the wedding service in German. "Bruders and Schwesterns, we are

151

ready to begin this wedding. William Boxholder, you lead the first hymn."

The song leader stood up. "Turn to page 378 in the Ausbund for *So will ichs aber heben an, Singen in Gottes Ehr (Singing in God's Honor)*. Pages rustled as people rifled through their hymn books, locating the song. Once the page was found, the room went silent. William Boxholder deep, clear voice began the song, and the rest joined in.

The next song leader, Nathan Fisher announced, "Now we will sing *Lob Lied*."

This song took at least fifteen minutes to sing through the sixth verse at a very slow pace. That gave the wedding party time to walk down the aisle. The bishop motioned for an usher to bring in the wedding party.

The attendants paired off. Levi Yoder took Katie Yost hand. Adam and Emma, holding hands, walked to their chairs. Noah and Jenny Yoder followed. In the seating arrangement as when they greeted the guests, Adam and Emma sat between their two attendants, facing each other.

On the third line of the song, Bishop Bontrager, Minister Yoder and Deacon Yutzy rose to their feet and walk back down the aisle and outside. They were going to use the porch for their council room.

Adam took Emma by the elbow, gave her a twitchy smile and helped her stand. They followed the ministers. On the north end of the porch, Adam and Emma sat on one bench provide for them, and the ministers on the one facing them.

The singers began the hymn's next chorus. Nathan's clear tenor voice projected the words, and the guests joined in. Emma wondered at the countless times she'd sang that song very slow- *Oh Father God, we praise Thee*. The long verses lasted close to five minutes each.

Emma looked at Adam and at the ministers somber faces. Now wasn't the time to concentrate on that song or any other thought. She sat at this moment with Adam in front of the ministers for a very serious reason. This was part of their wedding ceremony.

Bishop Bontrager cleared his throat and counseled in a very serious tone. "You are taking a serious step this day to become man and wife, Adam Keim and Emma Lapp. I take it you have thought about this for some time."

The couple nodded agreement.

Luke Yoder, minister and friend, turned his attention on Emma. His friendly, easy going demeanor was gone, replaced with a solemn expression. His clear blue eyes seemed to probe deeply into her soul. "It has been told to you that no divorce is allowed. Once you marry Adam Keim it will be for life. Do you agree to this commitment for the rest of your life, Emma Lapp?"

"Jah, I do," Emma answered quietly.

"Do you agree to this commitment for the rest of your life, Adam Keim?" The bishop asked.

Adam nodded.

Deacon Yutzy asked Emma, "Have you remained pure for this marriage union?"

"Jah."

"Adam, have you remained pure?"

Adam nodded.

The Bishop looked from Adam to Emma and back to Adam. "Are you ready and willing to marry this woman today?"

"I am," Adam wrote on his notepad.

The bishop focused on Emma. "Are you ready and willing to marry this man this day?"

"I am," she replied.

The bishop bowed his head and blessed the couple with a prayer. "May God be the center of your marriage and bless you both with many happy years together. Amen."

Preacher Yoder and Deacon Yutzy echoed, "Amen."

The ministers stood up.

"Gute. Go back inside. We will be in shortly to get the service started," Luke said, shaking hands with Adam and Emma.

After the couple's dismissal, the ministers had to decide among themselves who would take the different parts of the wedding service. While they did that, Adam and Emma walked back down the aisle to their seats.

The Lob Lied song's sixth chorus was the ministers cue their time was up. They entered the house and took their places. Bishop Bontrager sat down in the middle chair between Luke Yoder and Enos Yutzy, and they joined in the singing.

After the song was over, Preacher Luke Yoder stood, tall and straight, to give his sermon. He looked around the gathering. "I greet all you in the name of Jesus Christ. I want to talk today about how God created Eve as a companion to Adam. Wives should learn from Eve's mistakes and not yield to temptation as she did. We find the responsibility of parenthood shown with the example of Cain and Abel. There are consequences of the sons of God taking daughters of men. I remind you that the bible shows us the fact that Noah and his sons only had one wife each." To end his sermon, Preacher Yoder bowed his head. "Let us have a silent prayer. All will kneel."

The congregation stood up and turned around. They knelt and leaned over their benches. When the prayer was over, the congregation stood, but they didn't turn around.

Deacon Enos Yutzy stood up with a bible in his hands and moved forward. "I will read scripture from Matthew 19." He opened the bible at a marker. "The Pharisees also came unto him, tempting him, and saying unto him, 'Is it lawful for a man to put away his wife for every cause?'

And he answered and said unto them, 'Have ye not read, that he which made them at the beginning made them male and female,' and said, 'For this cause shall a man leave father and mother, and shall cleave to his wife, and they twain shall be one flesh. What therefore God hath joined together, let not man put asunder.'

They say unto him, 'Why did Moses then command to give a writing of divorcement, and to put her away?'

He saith unto them, 'Moses because of the hardness of your hearts suffered you to put away your wives, but from the beginning it was not so.' And I say unto you, 'Whosoever shall put away his wife for fornication, and shall marry another, committeth adultery, and who so marrieth her which is put away doth commit adultery.'

His disciples say unto him, 'If the case of the man be so with his wife, it is not good to marry.'

But he said unto them, 'All men cannot receive this saying, save they to whom it is given."

Deacon Yutzy closed his bible and sat down. Then the guests turned around and sat down.

Bishop Bontrager stood up to give the main sermon. "Men, if you have wasted the years until now, there is no time to lose. Start cultivating a personal walk with Jesus Christ. Spend time regularly studying the scriptures and learning from them how God wants you to live your life and discharge your responsibilities to your wives.

Begin consulting Him about everything. If you are involved in an unhappy marital situation, the damage can be repaired, but the place to begin is with this matter of daily involvement with the person of Jesus Christ. Other efforts will fail until our hearts are right with Him, and we are growing in His likeness.

In the bible, we find Ruth and Boaz were both ready for marriage. So we turn from their spiritual preparation to their sterling courtship. Naomi and Ruth arrived in Bethlehem. The problem facing them was how to find enough food to eat. God had made a gracious provision in the Mosaic Law for folks in their predicament. Farmers were not permitted to reap the corners of their grain fields nor gather the gleanings. They left them for the poor, for foreigners, for widows and orphans.

Almost any way you look at it, Naomi and Ruth were qualified. They were poor widows, and Ruth was a foreigner. Since Naomi was getting a little too old to work in the fields, Ruth asked if she might go find the field of some kind man who would allow her to glean it. Naomi gave her permission. So Ruth departed and gleaned in the field after the reapers. She happened to come to the portion of the field belonging to Boaz, who was of the family of Elimelech.

The work was not easy—stooping and bending all day long as Ruth gathered the grain into her long, flowing cloak. The burden got heavier with each stalk she gleaned. The sun beat down on her back in that semi-tropical climate. A few of the bigoted hometown folks taunted her because of her foreign accent. Some of the men tried to put their hands on her. Every impulse in Ruth's body urged her to flee to the purple mountains of Moab which she could see in the distance. That was her home; that was where she belonged. But with quiet courage, simple modesty, and total unselfishness, she labored on.

We fully expect Boaz to notice her, and he did. "Whose young woman is this?" He asked his servant who was in charge of the reapers. "She is the young Moabite woman who returned with Naomi from the land of Moab," he replied.

Boaz lost no time in doing some nice things for Ruth. He invited her to stay in his fields and glean as much as she wanted. He said she was to drink freely from the water pitchers provided for his own workers.

Nowhere does it say that Ruth was a beautiful woman like Sarah, Rebekah, or Rachel. We do not know whether she was or not, but we do know she had an inner beauty, a meek and quiet spirit, an unpretentious humility that made her one of the loveliest women in scripture.

She bowed low before Boaz in genuine gratitude and said, "Why have I found favor in your sight that you should take notice of me, since I am a foreigner?" Her humility was evident again when she said, "You have comforted me and indeed have spoken kindly to your maidservant, though I am not like one of your maidservants."

There was nothing put on about Ruth. She was real. And her genuine humility, her meek and quiet spirit is one of the most valuable assets a woman can have. Peter says it is of great value in God's sight. It is a good trait for Christian women to ask God to help them develop.

Emma Lapp reminds me of Ruth. Not because of a quiet spirit," the bishop said and winked at Emma. That caused many in the congregation that knew Emma to snicker. The bishop continued, "But because Emma possesses humility, grace and courage of women much older than she is.

Boaz became more interested in lovely Ruth as the day went on. At mealtime, he invited her to join him and his reapers for lunch. He made sure she was served all she wanted to eat. When she finished eating and got up to return to work, Boaz said to his servants, "Let her glean even among the sheaves, and do not insult her. Also, you shall purposely pull out for her some grain from the bundles and leave it that she may glean easier, and do not rebuke her. So Ruth continued to glean until evening. When she beat out what she'd gleaned, she had nearly a bushel of barley.

Boaz was a kind man, thoughtful, considerate, and gentle. These are Christ-like traits. These are good traits for Christian men to ask God to help them develop. Like Boaz, I see these traits already in Adam Keim.

Well, it was time to make a move to show a couple would like to marry. In that culture, it was the woman's move to make. Naomi told Ruth exactly how to make her move on Boaz. Ruth listened carefully and carried out her instructions precisely. Boaz slept on the threshing floor that night to protect his grain from thieves. After he went to sleep; Ruth tiptoed in, uncovered his feet, and laid down. By this act she was requesting Boaz to become her goel.

Needless to say, Boaz was somewhat startled when he rolled over in the middle of that dark night and realized there was a woman lying at his feet. Unable to see Ruth well enough to recognize her, he asked, "Who are you?"

She answered, "I am Ruth your maid. So spread your covering over your maid."

Spreading his cloak over her signified his willingness to become her protector and provider. His response was immediate: "May you be blessed of the Lord. You have shown your last kindness to be better than the first by not going after young men, whether poor or rich. Now do not fear. I will do for you whatever you ask. For all my people in the city know you are a woman of excellence."

In the secluded darkness of the threshing room, Boaz could

have gratified his human desires, but he was a godly, moral, self-disciplined, Spirit-controlled man. He kept his hands off Ruth, and she slept at his feet until morning.

Furthermore, Ruth had the reputation of being a woman of excellence. She was able to claim God's grace and strength to hold herself in check until marriage.

Boaz and Ruth both knew God's greatest blessing in marriage required purity before marriage. Carelessness in this area would bring guilt, loss of self-respect, and suspicion. And it could leave scars on their souls that would make their adjustment to each other in marriage most difficult.

Boaz and Ruth did it God's way. We are not surprised to see their successful marriage. Their marriage was richly blessed by God.

Now that Ruth had her husband, she could have resented her former mother-in-law as an intruder. But when a person is filled with the love of God, his or her heart is big enough to engulf more than just one special person, or even a special few. She tenderly and unselfishly reaches out to meet the needs of others as well. It is striking to observe how God's love in Ruth's life overcame all obstacles—poverty, racial prejudice, age disparity, physical temptations and taking care of her mother-in-law.

I see in Adam Keim and Emma Lapp all the wonderful qualities of Boaz and Ruth. They will be a blessing to themselves, their children and their extended family.

It is never too soon to learn these lessons of love. We can begin teaching them to our children very early in their lives. The training ground for love is the home. A loving relationship with parents and brothers and sisters will prepare them to love their mates and their mates' parents as they should as it did for Adam and Emma.

Children will not know how to love when they marry unless they show love to those with whom they live right now. But it all begins with our love for the Lord. When we have experienced the love of God, we will express it in our family relationships—parents, bruders, schwesterns, husbands, wives, children, and in-laws.

Ruth was ready for a beautiful love affair with Boaz, because she was in love with her Lord. That love spilled out to others in her life.

We all must remember the husband has the major responsibility of directing the home for the glory of Christ. He needs to have the proper relationship with Christ in submission and self denial to glorify his Head. His is the God delegated authority over the submissive woman and is responsible for her actions in the home and in society.

Husbands love your wives, even as Christ also loved the church, and gave himself for it."

Emma glanced behind her when she heard the rustle at the back of the tent. The kitchen helpers slipped along the wall to the doorway as quietly as they could. They knew when the bishop was almost through with the sermon. It would soon be time for the vows. This was the helpers cue to get back to work so the meal would be done in time.

The sound of the bishop's voice brought Emma back to his story. She tried to stay calm as the bishop looked down at Adam and her. She knew the service was about over. The next part was the wedding ceremony when Adam and she said their vows in front of everyone. All eyes would be on them. She clasped her trembling hands tightly together. As nervous as she was she hoped she didn't do or say anything wrong during her vows.

Chapter 14

"We have two people here before us who have agreed to enter into the state of matrimony, Adam Keim and Emma Lapp. If it is still your desire to be married, Bruder and Schwestern, in the name of the Lord come forth," Bishop Bontrager commanded.

The couple stood up, joined hands and went to stand in front of the bishop.

Bishop Bontrager said, "Do you both still feel as you did earlier this morning when we talked about you getting married?"

"Jah," Emma said.

Adam reached for his notepad and pen.

The bishop said, "Adam, where it is proper you nod your head if you would like?"

Adam nodded yes.

"Fine, Adam. Now we have here two people who have agreed to enter the state of matrimony, Adam Keim and Emma Lapp. Those here to witness this wedding today speak now if you know of any scriptural reason why these two people cannot be married. You should let yourself be heard now or forever remain silent."

After a pause, the bishop said, "No one has any objection." He opened his bible and quoted from the book of Ephesians 5:22-33. "Husbands love your wives, even as Christ also loved the church, and gave himself for it. For this cause shall a man leave his father and mother and shall be joined unto his wife, and they shall be one flesh."

The bishop joined his hands over the top and bottom of Adam and Emma's hands. He asked both of them, "Can you both confess and believe that God has ordained marriage to be a union between one man and one wife, and do you also have confidence you are approaching marriage in accordance with the way you have been taught?"

Emma answered, "Jah."

Adam nodded yes.

"Adam Keim, do you have confidence, Bruder, that the Lord has proved this, our schwestern as a marriage partner for you?"

Adam shook his head emphatically yes.

"Gute, Adam. Emma Lapp, do you have the confidence, schwestern, that the Lord has provided this, our bruder, as a marriage partner for you?"

"Jah."

"Adam, do you promise your wife that if she should in bodily weakness, sickness or any similar circumstances need your help that you will care for her as a fitting Christian husband?"

Adam nodded yes.

"Emma, do you promise your husband if he should in bodily weakness, sickness or any similar circumstances need your help, that you will care for him as is fitting for a Christian wife?"

"Jah," Emma said.

Bishop Bontrager asked both of them, "Do you both promise together that you will with love, forbearance and patience live with each other, and not part from each other until God will separate you with death?"

The couple nodded their heads, and Emma said, "Jah."

Bishop Bontrager let go of their hands. "Let's pray."

After the prayer, the bishop took Emma's hand and placed it in the hand of Adam. With his hands covering theirs for the blessing, he quoted from the book of Tobit. "And he takes the

161

hand of the daughter and puts it in the hand of Tobias. The God of Abraham and the God of Isaac and the God of Jacob be with you and help you together and give his blessings richly unto you.

I wish you the blessings of God for a gute beginning and a steadfast middle time, and may you hold out until a blessed end. This all in and through Jesus Christ. Amen."

At the mention of Christ, all three bent their knees.

Bishop Bontrager said, "Go forth in the name of the Lord. I say you are now man and wife, and may the Lord bless you with his everlasting love."

Adam looked relieved. Emma's face radiated a blissful glow. The couple joined hands and returned to their seats. The bishop asked Preacher Yoder and Deacon Yutzy to express their thoughts on the wedding ceremony. They each took a few minutes to wish the couple God's blessings. After the two men finished, the bishop asked the bride's father, John Lapp, to say a few words.

John stood. "This is a very special occasion to now have a new member in our family. Hal and I have looked forward to this day for a long time. We sometimes thought it would never come. Now we look forward to being a part of this couple's life." He paused to glance at Hal, and she winked at him.

"Thanks to all who helped work so hard to get prepared for the wedding. The Lapp family appreciated their work. It has been a blessing to have Hal's mother, father and aunt here to help us during this busy time. We have enjoyed their company, appreciated their help and feel blessed that they could be here to witness this joyous occasion with us.

Hal and I sincerely wish our daughter, Emma, and her new family a blessed and happy life."

John sat down, and Bishop Bontrager stood. "Amos Keim, Adam's uncle, will now say a few words in place of Bobby and Adam's late father, Elmo Keim."

Amos stood. "The Keim family is blessed to have Emma as part of it. We will ever be thankful to God for bringing Emma and Adam together to enrich our family."

162

Next the bishop asked the congregation to kneel in prayer. Everyone stood, turned to face their bench and knelt.

The bishop read the prayer out of the Christenpflicht prayer book as it is done at the close of Amish worship services. The prayer was a little long. The bishop chose the prayer, because he expected the ceremony to be somewhat shorter than it turned out. Since he picked the prayer before hand, the bishop didn't want to exchange it now for a shorter one at the last minute.

The congregation rose but remained facing backward for the benediction. Then they turned around for one more hymn, and the wedding ceremony ended at midday. Time for people to leave the house and get in line to be ushered into the tent. There was still a lot more celebration to go.

Several of the young people left the house before the bridal party to help with the preparations for dinner by being waitresses and waiters. With a good size crowd like this one, it took two waiters and eight waitresses for the tent.

Three young married couples, the *eck leit* or corner people, were assigned just to wait on the bridal party seated in the corner.

The cooks didn't get to see much of the wedding service. Four married couples were assigned as cooks. Most of the morning, they stayed with the food they were preparing. Three married couples were in charge of cooking the potatoes and warming other dishes.

Once she was outside, Tootie stood off to the side and watched as people filed out of the house. Somehow she had gotten separated from Nora and Hal. With so many people coming out of the house single file, it was going to take awhile. It didn't take her long to decide she needed a place to sit down. She might as well go inside the tent and get out of the sun. She'd catch up with her sister and Hal later.

Tootie blinked a few times, trying to get her eyes adjusted to the dim lighting. Plenty of benches to sit on. She headed along the wall to the corner at the front of the tent. She sat on the end of the last bench before the corner. That should put her out of the way when everyone else came in for the meal.

The tables already had plates, silverware and coffee cups at each seating place. Tootie tapped the plate in front of her. A real one. That surprised her. She expected to eat off paper plates with this many people to feed. She hoped there was plenty of assigned dishwashers. She'd hate to have to hide out after lunch to keep from doing dishes.

A cake or pie set every three feet apart on the tables. Tootie was impressed. What work the bakers went to, baking this many pies and cakes. She studied the crust covered pie three plate settings down from her and hoped it one she could eat. Raspberries were too seedy for her dentures, and gooseberries had too much acid in them for her delicate stomach. She'd hate to make the Amish guests sitting near her mad by turning down a dessert. It might be the very woman who baked the pie.

Suddenly, Adam's Uncle Amos Keim, taking the place of the groom's father, came in and was followed by a continuous line of men. They followed along the wall, headed right for Tootie.

Amos nodded at her as he sat beside her. When the benches on that side were filled, men sat down on the opposite side of the table across from Tootie and on to the end of that row of tables.

John Lapp and Emma's brother, Daniel, were among the group of men seated at the first table along the wall. Across from them several older Amish men, the church elders, sat. Men continued coming in single file and filled up seats on the right side of the other tables.

After the men were seated at those tables, the women came in single file and sat across from the men. There was no specific order. The women didn't sit with their spouse or family. They took whatever seat was next.

Tootie noticed the tables along the wall was the only row of tables that had just men sitting at it. She was embarrassed to see she picked the wrong place to sit, an English woman among all those Amish men. She'd been so busy she hadn't had time to read the chapter on wedding receptions in the special occasions Amish book she brought with her. Clearly, she should have made time. Oh, well, too late now. She was trapped in place.

After relatives and guests were seated, the bride and groom and their attendants came in. The eck corner was where Adam and Emma headed with the other couples in the bridal party. The couple sat across the corner from each other, with Emma on Adam's left.

On that table was a beautiful wedding cake made by the Weber sisters, with golden honeysuckles on it but not any other decorations. There was a lovely glass pitcher filled with water and hand painted glasses on display near the cake.

There were tables for Amish boys but only a few Amish girls joined them since most of the girls were servers. Smaller children like Redbird and Beth were in the kitchen with the helpers.

Shortly after everyone was seated, the clock chimed noon. Everyone bowed their head in silent prayer. It seemed like that prayer was a long one. Tootie's stomach growled. Embarrassed, she pressed her arm tightly to her stomach, sure the white haired man, sitting so close to her, must have heard the rumble. She wished for the prayer to end. All of a sudden, everyone lifted up their head and started talking.

At this point, the waitresses came in with bowls of coleslaw, and creamed peas. They all brought in the same item to serve at the same time. After the slaw and peas came chicken gravy, mashed potatoes, fried chicken, fresh bread, butter and jelly.

Amos Keim gave Tootie a friendly smile. "Are you enjoying the wedding?"

"Very much," Tootie replied.

Soon Tootie's plate was full. A waitress came around with coffee. Tootie said, "I hate to be a bother, but could you just put water in my cup? I usually drink water for lunch."

"Sure, you can have water," said the waitress. She brought Tootie a glass of water.

As soon as one bowl of food was empty another one was carried in to take its place.

Amos Keim noticed how fast Tootie was eating the food on

her plate. "Are you enjoying the food?"

"Everything is delicious. Best mashed potatoes, gravy and fried chicken I've ever eaten. The potatoes are so creamy and fluffy," Tootie told him. "When do they bring in the creamed celery?"

Amos thought about that a second. "I never see creamed celery at a wedding."

"I was sure I read in my Amish book celery was used as part of the wedding menu," Tootie said, thinking this friendly fellow had pretty blue eyes.

"Maybe somewhere else," he said. "Celery does not grows gute here in Iowa."

Hal and her mother sat together, and Tootie should have been with them. Nora looked down the line of women seated at their table. "I can't pick out Tootie. Have you seen her?"

Hal glanced around. "I haven't. Uh oh."

"What?" Nora asked.

"Mom, she's at the first table with the men up next to the eck."

"Now why on earth would she sit there with the men?" hissed Nora.

"Don't get upset, Mom. No one cares. They understand that Tootie isn't used to how we sit at a wedding."

Nora grinned. "Here we go again. She seems to be having a friendly conversation with Adam's uncle. I just hope she doesn't try to talk him into going for a ride in the courting buggy with her."

Hal whispered behind her hand, "She does seem to have developed an attraction for Amish men, doesn't she?"

"Funny isn't it? For a woman who thinks she is an expert on Amish customs, she sure flubbed this one up."

"Maybe not, Mom. Aunt Tootie may have sat there on purpose with all those men," Hal said, smiling.

Nora frowned at her daughter. "Hallie, I don't find that one bit funny." She focused on Tootie giving the elderly man a sweet smile. "Is Adam's uncle married?"

"Yes."

"Good, that takes care of that problem, I hope," Nora said, sounding relieved. "Who is that man about four seats down from John that looks so much like him?"

"That's Marvin, John's brother. You will have to meet Marvin's five year old twin sons. They look just like Marvin and John. After lunch, I will introduce you to all the relatives."

After the meal, the Ausbund hymn books were passed around for singing. These books have no musical notes but are strictly words written in old German. One of the young men started singing a song then the others joined in. This went on for some time.

Tootie listened, but she had no idea what they were singing so she couldn't sing along. The singing was peaceful and lovely, and Tootie had a full stomach. She'd ate more than she usually did and still made room for the pie. She was delighted to find out it was pumpkin, one of her favorites.

The music made Tootie really mellow. She liked this feeling that she was part of the Amish world. As she concentrated on the music, Tootie's head nodded. She jerked back up and blinked her heavy eye lids. She nodded off again.

All of a sudden, everyone stopped singing. The tent was quiet for a moment. Then the only sounds in the room were small cooking pots rattling with coins in them and Tootie loud rumbling snores.

Adam's smaller cousins jingled their pans at the far end of Tootie's table expecting donations.

Nora was beside herself as she hissed, "Oh, Hallie, how embarrassing. Can't John or your father wake Tootie up right quick?"

"They are both too far away, and Adam's Uncle Amos isn't going to be any help. Look at him grin at her. He thinks this is funny."

Emma was looking around the room as was everyone else to see where the snoring came from. Adam grinned as he elbowed Emma and nodded toward Tootie.

Emma giggled as she put her hand over her mouth. She whispered, "Poor Aendi Tootie. She has worked hard the last few days and getting up early has gotten the best of her. I hope she goes to bed earlier tonight. She needs to take care of herself and get plenty of rest."

Adam grinned at Emma and wiggled a finger between the two of them. He was trying to say they should be in bed early, too. The thought was enough to make her blush.

The two boys jingled their pans noisily. One of the boys finally stood next to Tootie. The tinny sounds woke Tootie up. She rubbed her eyes and stared at the boy a minute. Then she turned to Amos. "What does the boy want?"

"He is taking up a collection to share among the women who helped in the kitchen. Everyone only puts a few coins in. That's all."

Tootie said, "I didn't bring any money out here with me." She whispered to the boy, "I'll catch up with you later."

Once the collection ended, the men stood up and started out the door single file, followed by the women. The young girls that served the food came to the tables. They reached underneath and pulled out two dish pans, soap, dish towels and dish cloths. The girls set everything up at the end of the table to do the dishes.

Time for me to get out of here before they find out I'm Emma's Aunt and ask me to help do dishes. I don't remember exactly, but that might be one of the duties of the aunt, Tootie thought. She skipped over into the line of women and followed the last of the men out as she watched the dish washers getting organized.

Once outside, Tootie turned and looked back into the tent. A girl stacked the dishes. One washed, and one rinsed. Another one towel dried. Others wiped the tables and set the clean dishes back in place for the evening meal. Tootie was impressed at how fast they worked. With all that help, they had the routine of dish washing down pat. They didn't needed her after all.

Women passed by Tootie with more cakes and pies to replace the ones eaten for dessert. They were placed on the tables for the evening meal.

Nora slipped up behind Tootie, peeking in the tent. "What are you doing?"

"Watching the workers. It takes a lot of women working together to cook and clean up for a large wedding. They just set the tables again for the evening meal with clean dishes. I sure hope most of those women stick around afterwords. Otherwise, according to my book, *The Amish Wedding and other special occasions of the Old Order Communities,* you and I are in charge. If they leave too early, you and I might get stuck with washing a ton of dishes."

"For Pete's sake, Tootie, stop worrying. Reading that book hasn't done you much good so far, otherwise you wouldn't have wound up eating with the men." Tootie opened her mouth to make an excuse, but Nora kept talking. "Now get away from this door and out of the workers way. Let them do their jobs." Nora grabbed Tootie by the arm and led her over to a group of women Hal was with.

During the social time, Adam and Emma walked around through the guests, talking to as many of them as they could. To the men that were interested, Adam offered thin cigars the size of cigarettes. The rest of the guests, Emma offered ballpoint pens for a remembrance. On the side of the pen was written Faith and Love, Adam and Emma Keim, September 15, 2014.

The children were given Snickers candy bars.

When the cleanup was over, women moved back into the tent to sit down and visit. The men stood in the yard. The younger children ran off to play a game of softball. The teenagers separated, the girls to Emma's room upstairs to visit, and the boys by the barn to play darts.

Hal searched the crowd for Emma. "Your wedding gifts are on the bed in the spare room. Are you ready to come upstairs and open them."

"Sure."

Hal announced to the women in the tent, "Come with us. Emma's going to open her gifts."

As soon as they reached the spare bedroom, Emma sat down

on the bed in the middle of the gifts and waited for the women to fill the room.

As Emma opened the gifts, she found new and practical items. In a few minutes, stacked Tupperware containers, crystal salad and fruit bowls and kitchen utensils covered the bed. A special gift came from John and Hal. It was a cast iron waffle maker which Emma knew Adam would be pleased with.

Each gift had a slip of paper attached with a pin to the wrapping so Emma knew who gave her the gift. She opened a large gift and ran her hand over the quilt she'd helped put together at the quilting frolic. The milky way quilt made by Mammi Nora and Aendi Tootie.

"Mammi and Aendi Tootie, this is so beautiful. You out did yourself putting together this lovely quilt. So much hard work went into it."

"It was a labor of love," Nora said.

"One that made us nervous until we finished it," Tootie added. "We aren't as efficient at quilt making as the rest of you are."

"We'd still be quilting on it if we hadn't had help from the ladies at the quilt frolic," Nora admitted. "I'm so glad Hal organized that so you ladies could help finish the quilt."

"All of you that quilted this lovely quilt, denki for putting in all that hard work for Adam and me," Emma said to the women. "Denki for your thoughtfulness and for all the wedding gifts. Each one will be a special reminder of you when I use them."

Hal joined John again as soon as the gift opening was over. John nodded to a group of women going back to the tent. "See my schwesterns. Let's say hello." When John and Hal caught up with his sisters, John greeted, "It is so voonderball gute, Beth and Amy, to see you today."

Beth, the slim and wiry sister, gave him a hug. "We would not have missed this wedding for anything in the world. Would we, Amy?" She gave Hal a hug and patted her back.

"Ach, nah!" said Amy, the plump one. She stood on tiptoes to hug her brother than Hal. "It is gute to see Emma so happy."

"John and I agree, and we are so proud to have Adam be a part of the Lapp family," Hal assured them. "Denki to both of you for all your hard work, cleaning the windows and house. We so appreciated it. I don't have to fear spiders or dust for awhile, and I can actually see who is coming when I look out of the windows."

The sisters giggled behind their hands.

Amy said, "You are wilcom."

Beth turned serious. "John, have you had time to talk to our bruder, Marvin, today."

"We had a gute visit early this morning," John said. "And we visited some during lunch when we sit together."

"Voonderball gute! Ida sit with Amy and me so we could visit. Will you let us know when we can bring Marvin and Ida to visit you while they are here," Beth said excitedly.

Hal said. "I'm hoping they stay long enough to visit around the neighborhood. As far as we're concerned, you should come for meals any time you want and spend as much time as you can with us while they're here. We will be glad to have all of you any time. Just come."

"Denki, Schwestern Hal. We will look forward to that," Amy said. "It has been a long time since we last had a family gathering with Marvin and his family. Ain't so, John? I can't remember how long. When do you think, Beth?"

"Right after the twins, John and Marvin, were born five years ago. Remember, we paid a driver to take us to see the new babies."

"That's right," Amy agreed.

Chapter 15

Daylight left as did most of the guests after the evening meal was over. Kerosene lamps were lit in the tent. The flames flickered on the shadowed walls. Winding down after a long day, the Lapp family visited with John's sisters, brother and their families.

Adam wrote on his notepad, "It is time to leave."

Emma sighed. "Just give me a few more minutes."

Now that the time had come, nervousness fluttered inside the new bride. She walked out of the tent and strolled across the yard. Under the maple tree, she stopped to take in the nearly cleared off garden. For years, she'd worked hard in that garden to produce food for her family. Now it would be Hal and the boys' job.

Emma surveyed the roadside stand Noah and Daniel just put up for another season. It was time for her brothers to fill the stand with squash and pumpkins. That stand had always been her project.

She walked back of the house. The martins had roosted in their houses for the night. The air smelled of sweetness from yellow and gold flowers on the honeysuckle vine climbing the trellis under her window. She loved the way the flowers made her room smell on summer evenings and the second blooming in early fall.

Once she settled in with Adam, she'd come back and get a start of the vine to put ... . Where would she put it? She didn't know where she was going? Adam hadn't told her yet. Was it to live with his mother and brother? Had he by some miracle and help from Bobby built the apartment above the furniture shop?

Emma would have to struggle hard to resist asking. She had to wait until Adam showed her tonight. She understood why. He was making her wait, because she was a doubting Thomas. She'd have felt so much better leaving her childhood home if she knew where she was going. Not that she had a choice. Now that they were married, she'd live where Adam lived even if it was in his horse barn.

She wandered through the mudroom and stopped in the kitchen by the wood cookstove. She sure hoped Daed was right about Hallie doing all right on her own. She would say some prayers for Hallie to be ready for full time housekeeping. She wouldn't have a choice. Hopefully, Mammi and Aendi Tootie stayed awhile longer. They could help Hallie adjust.

Emma walked slowly up the stairs to her bedroom. She took a deep breath to push back tears as she looked around. She'd never be sleeping in this room again. This place had been her safe haven under her daed's roof. Would she be comfortable and have a room that she could get away to be by herself in where Adam was taking her? Emma sat down on the bed and leaned forward with her head in her hands.

Adam followed Emma as far as the porch. He paced back and forth, waiting for her as she disappeared back of the house. He didn't see Hal until she tapped him on the shoulder.

"Where is the bride?"

He wrote, "Emma wanted a few minutes alone. She looked sad about leaving."

Adam's concern caused Hal to give him a comforting hug. Emma had put him through a lot. Adam was naturally going to be nervous, wondering what his new bride might do next. "Don't worry. Emma is feeling like every young bride does on her wedding day. I'll talk to her and hurry her up."

Hal walked around the house. Emma wasn't in sight. She decided to check upstairs in Emma's bedroom. That's where she often found Emma when she wanted to be alone.

When Hal opened the door, the hinges squeaked. Emma sat up straight. Hal sat on the bed beside her. "Adam's waiting for you, and not so patiently I might add. Was ist letz?"

Emma rubbed the quilt on the bed. "Nothing is the matter. I am just looking around one last time. Saying gute bye to the days of my childhood and feeling a little surprised that I have suddenly become a woman."

"You certainly have. It seems you grew up way too fast. Now don't look so sad, or you'll make me sad. When I get sad, I cry, and you don't want that. It's not like you're moving a long ways off. Three miles is close, and it's with Adam for goodness sakes."

"I know, but it is not the same as being here with you and the family every minute where I can see what is going on."

Hal assured her, "You can come visit any time of day or night. You know that. I expect you to. If you need help with anything just ask."

"I'm going to miss you and Daed and the boys."

"That's only natural. We're going to miss you, but now you have a new life with Adam."

"Jah, I just wish I knew what the beginning was going to be like. I want to know where we are going to live. Adam has not told me. If I had not made him so mad, I would know already I suppose." Emma paused then said, "We really should spend the night here like most newly married couples so we can help with clean up tomorrow."

Hal took Emma's hand and squeezed it. "You know Adam wants you to go with him. Do what Adam wants. You can trust him. Let me tell you, I expect you back tomorrow bright and early to help clean up. That will be an all day job."

"I want to trust Adam, but where are we going to live," Emma repeated.

"Trust me when I say Adam knows what he's doing," Hal insisted, squeezing Emma's hand.

Emma studied Hal. "Do you know where Adam is taking me?"

Hal wrinkled her nose and said slowly, "Jah."

Emma asked brusquely, "Have you known all the time?"

"Ach, nah! Honest, Emma. Not until last night. I was as worried as you are, so I insisted John tell me. If I didn't like his answer, I was going to insist Adam and you stay with us."

"Now that you know, tell me," Emma said in a low, urgent voice.

"I can't. John made me promise I wouldn't. It is what Adam wants, and it is for him to tell you."

Emma asked warily, "Am I going to like it?"

"Jah, you trust Adam to do the recht thing, and you will be all recht no matter what," Hal said evenly.

"Sure, I do know I must. Now I want to go to the chicken house and tell Abraham gute bye."

"Emma! You're stalling while you torture poor Adam. Tomorrow evening when you're ready to go home take Abraham and as many of the hens as you find you have room for. Just leave me a few hens for a start, and go with me to the salebarn some day to buy a new rooster."

"I would like that. We do need to hatch out more pullets, too. We're short on laying hens since I gave Ada Jostle some of ours." Emma gives her a hug. With a new found confidence that everything was going to work out all right because Hallie said so, Emma walked downstairs, out of the house and down the porch steps. Adam's eyes showed his concern. Emma took his hand. "Time to go, my husband."

After the couple drove off, Hal wiped tears. Nora put her arm around her daughter. "Years go by, and time seems to stand still. Suddenly, the children are grown and leaving home. Hallie, I know how you feel. I felt the same way the first time you left home. Takes some getting used to, but believe me, you will adjust. Just like I did."

From behind them, Tootie added, "According to my Amish book, that's repeated over and over again until you quit getting pregnant and have all the kids raised."

"Tootie, honestly!" Nora snapped at her.

"It's all right, Mom. Aunt Tootie's book is right," Hal said,

175

knowing that is the way it works for Amish women.

Once she was in the buggy, Emma was on pins and needles. She gripped her hands together in her lap and concentrated on the dark scenery. They passed the Bontrager farm, turned south at the intersection and went by the Yoder farm. Next was the Manwiller farm and the Jostle farm. The driveway to the Keim farm was coming up.

She liked Adam's mother, but it was going to feel strange working in another woman's kitchen. Lovina had her own way of doing things. Emma had to be careful to follow Lovina's lead where the kitchen was concerned. She'd manage since that would be Adam and her home for awhile.

Most brides spent a few months in their parents home until they got a place of their own. That would have been the most comfortable situation for Emma, but that wasn't what Adam had in mind. She had to make do with Lovina's house, because she loved him.

Adam drove passed the driveway. Emma grabbed his arm. "Adam, wake up? You just drove by your farm driveway. Turn around."

Adam nodded no. He slapped the horse's back and kept going.

"Do you know where you are going?"

He smiled and nodded yes.

Evidently, they weren't going to live with Lovina and Bobby. Emma thought she'd figured out where they would live. Adam did get the apartment above the shop ready. Emma didn't know how as busy as he was. Maybe the whole apartment wasn't finished yet. They would live in it while Adam found time to complete the rooms. That was all right. Just the two of them in the apartment was ideal to her way of thinking. Better than living with Lovina and Bobby. Of course, she'd have to get used to Priscilla in the shop under her every day. The differences between them, hopefully, would get easier as time went by.

Adam drove by the furniture shop driveway.

Emma twisted around and eyed the driveway in the tail lights red beams. Her curiosity kept mounting. "We are not going to live in the upstairs of the shop?"

Adam nodded sideways.

Emma opened her mouth to speak. Adam's left eyebrow arched in a warning. Emma leaned back and pressed her lips together tightly to help her remain silent. They passed the timber that bordered the shop. Adam pulled back on Sophie's lines to slow her down and turned the buggy into a field driveway.

"Ach, Adam, I cannot stay silent any longer. Why are we in your field full of shocks? I really think it is not a gute idea to camp out when the nights are so cool. We didn't bring sleeping bags or bedding with us. The coyotes roam every night, and all sorts of other wild animals that I do not want to sleep with." She glanced at the star speckled sky, hoping for clouds. "It might rain tonight which would not be gute."

Adam grinned, clearly enjoying himself, as he pointed ahead of them.

Emma squinted to see through the dark. A white house loomed up at the end of the field. "I do not remember anyone living here for a long time. After the house burnt years ago, alls that was left were the outbuildings. Funny, I do not remember hearing that someone built a house behind this field. Who lives here?"

Adam pulled on Sophie's lines to stop her. He climbed out of the buggy and came around to Emma's side. His strong hands studied her as he lifted her down. "You are not going visiting this time of night. The house is dark. Those poor people are in bed. There will be plenty of days in the future for us to go visiting."

"They will not mind," Adam wrote.

Emma held the note pad close to make out the words by the buggy headlight. She was never going to figure Adam out if he kept doing such strange things. She hoped Hal knew what she was talking about when she said to trust this new husband.

Adam turned off the headlights and took Emma by the arm.

He led her up the porch steps. They paused at the door. Adam turned the knob. The door opened quietly into the dark kitchen. Emma whispered, "Adam, we cannot go in this house without knocking to let the owners know we are here."

Adam wrote on the notepad and handed it to Emma. She squinted at the paper and hissed, "It is too dark. I cannot read this."

Adam grabbed Emma's hand and led her inside. While she watched, he felt for a box on the table, struck a match and lit the kerosene lamp.

As the kitchen lit up, Emma tensed, waiting for someone to pounce into the kitchen and yell at them to leave. Her eyes grew wide as she kept a watch on the living room door.

Adam shook her hand with the note in it. Emma held the pad toward the light. "Your handwriting is terrible when you write in the dark. This looks like it says we can come in. We live here."

Emma was sure she'd misread the note. She read it again. Her eyes widened as she looked at Adam for clarification.

He nodded yes and smiled.

"In this brand new house?" Emma shrieked.

Adam nodded.

"Are you sure?"

Adam waved his hand toward the room, wanting her to look at the kitchen. Emma walked around, trying to take in the new smells of wood and fresh varnish. She had to get used to the wonder of it all. A light, wooden parquet floor, white painted walls and glowing pine cabinets were the kitchen of her dreams. A gas cookstove and refrigerator lined up with the counter.

Emma patted the gas stove, wondering how long it would take her to get used to cooking on it. Once she mastered it, she'd insist Hallie get a gas stove and help her learn to cook on it. When Hallie wanted one, Emma wouldn't give in. She was used to the wood cookstove, and now she didn't have a choice.

Above the door was a wooden plaque with a verse burnt into it. But as for me and my house, we will serve the Lord – Joshua

24:15.

In the middle of the kitchen was a long table with eight chairs around it. The dining set looked familiar. "This looks like the order you made for the English customer."

Adam nodded.

Emma leaned against the stainless steel sinks and folded her arms over her chest. "It seems to me, you did an awful lot of fibbing to pull this surprise off."

Adam wrote, "I did not say the furniture order was for an English customer. You decided that on your own."

Emma leveled a serious look at Adam. "All recht, I thought that is where the furniture would go. Is building this house what you were doing when everyone kept telling me you were busy?"

Adam nodded and motioned toward the living room door.

Emma walked into the next room. "You build this house by yourself?"

Adam wrote, "I had help from John, Jim and most of the men in the community."

Emma stopped to read again. "Is this where Daed, Dawdi and the boys went when he said they had to make Samuel Nicely's hay and to the salebarn?"

Adam nodded.

"No wonder Hallie and Mammi did not mind that Daed and Dawdi lied. As I recall now, Noah even gave me a hard time for not being more trusting of you."

He wrote, "It was hard to get the house built by myself in time for the wedding after the tornado destroyed so many places. In between helping rebuild storm damaged buildings, the men pitched in to help me."

"This is a wonderful surprise, but did you have to keep it from me for so long? Why did you let me worry that something was wrong with you? You knew I was upset."

Adam wrote, "I wanted it to be a surprise. A nice one I thought. I was ready to show you the house that Sunday when I asked you to go for a ride with me, but after you talked to me the way you did, I could not tell you about the house. I had to know you trusted me to do the recht things with blind faith, because you loved me. If you did not trust me now, you never would."

"That is what Bishop Bontrager told me. Tonight, Hallie said she was not going to let me go with you until she knew where we were going."

Adam's head went backward in surprise.

"Do not worry. Hallie gave Daed a hard time so he told her last night, but he made her promise not to tell me. All Hallie said tonight was I should trust you to do the recht thing. I gave her advice some thought, sitting on my bed in my old room for one last time." She paused, and Adam wavered his hand.

"I decided I loved you enough to marry you, Adam Keim. I want to spend the rest of my life with you. Even though I did not know what was ahead of me tonight. I had enough curiosity stored up in me to kill a cat, but I had to trust you.

Curiosity about so many things. Why you avoided me for weeks, and where we were going to live. I decided to do it your way and wait for you to show me and love where we lived even if it was in your horse barn. I realized I did not have a choice when your eyebrow kept going up if I spoke up."

Adam's chin came up, and his serious eyes never wavered from hers. They stared at each other for a moment so still it was as though time stopped.

Adam lifted an eyebrow, wanting Emma to go on. Amazed at her new found wisdom, she said, "After all my doubts, I was just thinking that life with you is worth living. I am stronger and wiser after being a doubting Thomas. Denki, for putting up with me and teaching me to trust you."

Emma held her arms out to Adam. He put his arms around her and pulled her close. She whispered in his ear, "I now know I can and will love you forever."

Amish Wedding Recipes
Courtesy of Patricia Brigode and Amish friends

Stuffing for an Amish Wedding

9 gallon toasted bread (15 big bread loaves)
1 ½ gallon potatoes, diced
1 ½ quart celery, chopped
1 ½ quart carrots, chopped
a little brown sugar
2 tbsp pepper
salt to taste
poultry seasoning
1 quart fresh parsley, chopped
1 quart onions, chopped
3 ½ gallons milk
2 quarts chicken pickings

Put stuffing in rectangular pans like cake pans or aluminum pans.

Bake at 335 for 40 to 45 minutes

Date Dessert

1 cup chopped dates
1 cup boiling water

Put dates in boiling water and let soak.

Mix together

1 ½ cups flour
½ tsp salt
½ cup sugar
1 ½ tsp. Baking soda
1 tsp. Margarine

Add soaked dates to the mixture and stir well.

Pour into 9 x 13 inch cake pan.

Mix brown sugar and 1 ½ cup boiling water and 1 TB. Margarine. Pour over batter in pan.

Bake 305 degrees for 40 – 45 minutes. Serve cold with cool whip.

Pecan Pie

Makes one pie

1 cup sugar
¼ cup Karo syrup
2 tsp. Margarine
¾ cup pecans
¼ tsp salt
3 eggs, beaten

Beat eggs well. Add sugar, salt, Karo syrup and margarine. Mix well. Put pecans in unbaked pie shell. Pour egg mixture over pecans.

Bake one hour at 350 degrees.

Takes 12 batches for a wedding.

Pumpkin Pie

Makes one pie

¾ cup brown sugar
½ tsp cinnamon
¼ tsp salt
1 cup pumpkin
3 eggs separated and (beat egg whites)
1 cup milk
1 tsp vanilla

Blend sugar, cinnamon, salt and pumpkin; stir in egg yolks, add milk and mix well; add beaten egg whites last. Pour into unbaked pie shell.

Bake in hot oven 425 degrees for 20 minutes, then reduce temperature to 350 degrees and bake 20 minutes or longer until done.

Emma's favorite butchering day cake.

Lard Cake

1&1/2 c. heavy cream
2&1/4 c. sour milk
2 heaping t. baking soda
3 eggs
3 or 4 c. all-purpose flour
1/2 t. salt
3 t. sugar and sugar for rolling

In a large mixing bowl, combine the cream, sour milk, baking soda, eggs and flour. The consistency should be similar to a pie dough, so add a little more flour if needed. Add salt and sugar. Roll out to 1/4-inch thickness and cut up in any shape as big as you wish, or into 2-by-4-inch pieces. Cut a 21/2-inch slit in the center of each cake. Make sure the slit goes completely through the cake. Then drop the cakes into a kettle of hot melted lard about two inches deep. Roll in a pan of sugar while still warm.

Amish Wedding Fried Chicken

Keep in mind this recipe for Amish chicken is intended for serving at an Amish wedding meal. So, it's made in extra large quantities and is enough for an Amish wedding dinner and supper.

We suggest that if you would like to try it, you may want to consider scaling back the amounts or even just use the basic idea - unless, of course, you have a large family, are having a big party, or just want a huge amount!

Ingredients:

140 lb. boneless chicken breast pieces
140 lb. boneless thighs

Breading Mix:

3 3/4 lb. Bisquick

1 1/4 lb. flaky crust flour

2 c. seasoning salt

1 Tbsp. Paprika

2 lb. Emma's chicken coating

Makes 3 batches. Fry in butter and canola oil.

Pour 2 c. water in large roaster. Line roaster with wire rack or tin foil. Fill with fried chicken. Bake at 275° for 2 hours.

Amish Wedding Fried Chicken

Option two

Gravy

1 c. butter, browned
2 c. flour
1/2 Tbsp. Lemon pepper
2 qt. Water
2 qt. chicken broth
2 pkg. gravy mix
5 slices Velveeta cheese

Make 4 batches for amount of chicken. Mix browned butter with flour. Add lemon pepper, water and chicken broth. Add gravy mix. Make according to directions on package. Add cheese. Melt into gravy and layer this with fried chicken pieces before you put them in the oven. Bake at 350° for 2 hours. This makes very moist chicken.

1 egg
3/4 cup cream
Pinch of salt
2 to 3 cups all purpose flour
Vegetable shortening or lard (for deep frying)
Powdered sugar (for sprinkling)

Beat the egg and stir in the cream, salt and enough flour to make a stiff, elastic dough. Divide the dough into 6 or 7 balls. Roll each ball flat and very thin (1/16-inch).Cut three 2-inch slits, one above the other, through the middle of each piece.

Heat shortening in a large kettle over high heat. When the shortening reaches 365 degrees F or a piece of dough tossed in sizzles, put one piece of dough at a time into the kettle. Turn each piece over with two forks when you see a slight golden color. Take out and put on a plate covered with paper towels to drain.

Sprinkle powdered sugar over the top. Stack all of the Nothings on one plate and serve.

For any of you readers that have started with Doubting Thomas in the Nurse Hal Among The Amish series, I thought you might like to have a peek at the very first book in the series.

A Promise Is A Promise
Excerpt from chapter one

Hal parked by the house. Without barking, Patches raced to meet her. She could tell he had missed her. The dog jumped upon her and licked her face. He bounced off Hal and did a dance, turning in circles. The curtains fluttered on the window. Emma burst from the house. Her face held a grateful expression. The girl's black skirt whipped around her legs as she rushed down the walk. Hal held out her arms and Emma rushed into them for a hug.

"I've done a lot of thinking about your father and what you said, Emma. I don't want to live the rest of my life alone when I could be a part of a wonderful family like yours. I'd like to talk to John," Hal said in a hushed voice.

"I am so glad," Emma said.

"Don't get your hopes up yet. He may be so hurt because I turned him down that he won't want anything to do with me," Hal warned her.

"Just try to talk to him," pleaded Emma.

."Where is he?"

"Fixing the hog pen fence last I noticed. The pigs got out again last night. I will go with you," Emma said.

Patches trailed at Hal's heels, unusually quiet as if he sensed impending doom. The north wind was freezing. A gust whipped at Hal's coat tail. She pulled her coat tighter together to ward off the winter chill. A rhythmical hammering came from close by. Just knowing that she was near John Lapp made the top of Hal's head light as her blood pressure shot up.

As Emma wrapped her coat around herself, she called, "Daed, where are you?"

"In the pig pen." John stood up, with his hammer poised in

189

his hand. He didn't move. With no expression at all on his face, John Lapp watched Hal and Emma came toward him. John keep his gaze level and indecipherable. His face was stony except for a quiver along his jar. He didn't look like he cared that Hal came to see him. He just waited.

Finally when she thought she had walked far enough with Hal, Emma stopped.

Hal walk on alone. When she was close enough to hear the pigs grunt and squeal as they chased after each other to keep warm, she knew her voice would carry on the wind without talking too loud. "Hello, John. Fixing the fence?"

"Yes," he said. His voice was tight and raspy. John dropped his hammer over the fence and climbed out of the pen. He stuck his hands in his pockets and kept his eyes on her face as he walked toward her. When he was within a few feet of her, he stopped as if he had no desire to get any closer.

Hal started. "Could we talk?"

John looked into her eyes. "I fear there is nothing left to say, but you are here for some reason so talk if you want."

Hal hadn't expected this meeting to be easy. At this range the hurt in his eyes was evident now as he studied her. Panic welled up in her. She was wasting her time. Hal's hands turned into tight fists at her sides. She tilted her head upward toward the gray, winter sky to avoid his eyes. She prayed she would say the right things to make John listen to her with an open mind. Thinking she might never find another chance at happiness, she took a deep breath and hoped the excess oxygen would help her collect her thoughts.

Hal was determined to be emotionally tough. She thought she would state her case and wait for John's answer. Now she found she couldn't control the urge to cry. Her eyes misted over and tears rolled down her cheeks. She couldn't take the slight tremble out of her voice. "I've given a lot of thought to us, John. I've missed you and the children so very much. Your family spoiled me in many ways. One thing I've learned has been I don't want to live the rest of my life alone."

Hal stopped to take another deep breath and focused on a

pillow like cloud floating above John's head. She didn't want to watch his unemotional face if he wasn't going to talk to her. She definitely didn't want to look into his agony filled, chocolate brown eyes. "I admit my pride got in the way when you proposed to me. As much as I wanted to be a part of your family, I expected you to share with me the family secret that has made all of you so unhappy. I wasn't sure I could be a part of this family if you didn't let me help you. When you didn't mention the secret that day in the sleigh, I thought you didn't trust me," she said honestly.

Hal wiped her eyes on her coat sleeve. She dared to take a look at John. He was watching her closely, but now she saw sympathetic warmth pooling in his dark eyes. It was a totally Amish, I feel sorry for you look. She completely lost it. "Oh, John. Stop looking at me with those eyes!"

In four steps, John was in front of her. He brushed a tear off her cheek with his thumb. With the back of his hands, he pushed her hair away from her face and tucked the strands back behind her ears. "You don't want me to look at you?"

"You're making me crazy."

"Is that good or bad?" John asked softly.

"Just let me finish what I have to say," Hal pleaded.

John put his hands down by his sides. He continued to watch her face. "Go on."

"I've had a lot of lonely time to think about the day you proposed. It doesn't matter to me anymore what happened in your past. I wasn't a part of your life back then. I'm asking you to forgive me for making you, me and the children miserable all this time." John's eyes narrowly focused on her. She couldn't tell what was going through his mind. "That's what I came to tell you. I was wrong to tell you I wouldn't marry you."

What made her feel as if her heart was about to break was the question he asked, "Why did you not come right out and ask me to tell you the secret that day? You have always been so direct before. It never dawned on me what was the matter with you. The more you became a part of my family, the less time we spent thinking about the secret. Being with you was what mattered to me and the children. Did you not feel that, Hal?"

"I did. I saw Emma feeling better, Noah coming out of his shell and Daniel enjoying my company. The children were turning more to me. I must admit, I wasn't sure where I stood with you. Your proposal surprised me, because it came out of the blue. Perhaps that's part of why I didn't give much thought to what I said," Hal excused.

John swallowed hard and said in a ragged voice, "All I could think was that you did not care enough about me to marry me. If I had only known what you were thinking. Can you understand I would have told you the whole story rather than risk losing you?"

Standing behind Hal, Emma sobbed loudly. Emma's upset. That's a bad sign, Hal thought. Emma must think my plea isn't going well with her father. Hal didn't want to bring up her promise to Emma, but it was the only thing she had left in her defense. "John, I couldn't ask you to tell me. I made a promise not to ask about the secret. I couldn't break that promise. At one time, I wanted to know the secret. I didn't know I was going to fall in love with you. Lately, I've had plenty of time to think. I've come to grips with this new and strange feeling called love that I didn't understand. Suddenly, I find nothing matters to me but your understanding and love. I don't have to know what happened if that is the way you want it. I can live without knowing. I don't intend to ask you now or ever again if you will have me for your wife."

"Oh my!" Emma cried out as she stepped up beside Hal. "This has all been my fault. I'm so sorry, Hallie."

"What is your fault?" John darted a concerned look at his upset daughter.

Ignoring her father, Emma fought to get control of her emotions as she pleaded with Hal, "Please forgive me."

"Sh! You don't have to say anything," Hal said, trying to stop her.

"What did Emma do?" John asked Hal, a baffled look on his face.

Emma and Hal concentrated on each other and ignored him.

Emma said to Hal, "Yes, I do. I had no idea that your promise to me was what has kept us apart. I release you from the promise. I would never want to do anything to keep you from being a part of our family."

"Don't you see? Knowing the secret isn't important to me any more. Being a part of your family is what is important. Us all being together is what is important," Hal insisted.

"Would you two talk to me? I'm right here," snapped John. Putting a hand on Emma and Hal's shoulders, he turned them to face him to get their attention.

"I'm so sorry, Daed." Emma agonized, wringing her hands. Her gray green eyes filled with the haunted sadness Hal remembered when they first met. "I could see the boys were getting so close to Hallie. It was only a matter of time before one of them confided in her. It is such a terrible secret, it weighed on Noah and Daniel. But I was afraid for Hallie to find out. If she did, she might leave us. I didn't want that so I told her to quit talking to the boys about Mom. She made a promise me that she would." Emma choked as she said, "Daed tell Hallie our awful secret. Tell her for all of us. Remember the verse in Corinthians. Just like Hallie, God keeps his promises. He will not allow us to be tested beyond our power to remain firm. When we are put to the test, he will give us the strength to endure and provide us with a way out. I'm going to the house to pray that Hallie still loves us enough to stay with us when she knows the awful truth."

Emma wiped the tears from her eyes as she raced back to the house.

"This doesn't have to be this way, John. I truly don't need to know if you don't want me to," Hal declared.

193

About The Author

Hello! I'm Fay Risner. I go by booksbyfay online. I enjoy writing about Amish life in the Nurse Hal Among The Amish series. As well as those books, I write a historical Amazing Gracie mystery series set in Iowa and Stringbean Hooper westerns. Also, I've written two books about Alzheimer's disease. I worked for many years in a nursing home and helped my mother care for my father which gave me insight about what caregivers deal with.

A romance such as *Christmas With Hover Hill* thrown into the mixture of books is a good way to switch genres. When an idea comes to me, I write the story.

Changing genres gives me flexibility as a writer. All my books are designed to offer some humor along with the serious moments. I write in 12 font to make my books reader friendly, and all my stories are suitable for any age group.

My husband and I live on an acreage with chickens, rabbits, cats and through the summer months a herd of goats. We enjoy raising a large garden and flowers. For fun, we go fishing in the summer and read a lot of books in the winter.

www.ingramcontent.com/pod-product-compliance
Lightning Source LLC
Chambersburg PA
CBHW071203260626
47162CB00003B/1155